I0621160

Exploring Deeper

ISBN: 978-1-7327260-0-0

Copyright © 2018

All rights reserved.

Table of Contents

Prologue

The Commander was locked in a battle of wills with her chief engineer. She could not allow him to undermine her authority.

"We've been over this, Commander. I'm not lighting this unless you use the magic words," repeated Puff, the engineer.

He continued to refuse, and everyone knew that the ship wasn't going anywhere unless Puff agreed to activate the interplanetary engines. The software was specifically designed to prevent everyone except the engineer and Commander from approving the boost away from Earth and toward their final lunar destination. The ship was on autopilot except for a few critical phases of flight where it asked permission to continue. This was one of those phases.

"Come on, Puff," sighed Olivia. "If we don't light this match, we're going to have to do a course correction and gravity assist at Mars that'll delay us by 2 months."

"Don't you worry, Olivia, I already knew that. But thanks for reminding our dear commander."

The rest of the crew groaned.

"Fine!" sighed the Commander. They had a three year mission ahead of them and she couldn't risk the mission for the sake of pride. Earth couldn't help her in this situation, and she knew that Puff was aware of that. The Commander had just never expected him to hijack the mission so early on, but she was also frustrated with herself for not having anticipated it. "Fine," she repeated.

The rest of the crew cranked their heads to listen to the Commander. All except for Puff who just stared at his switches and computer screens.

"Punch it, Chewie," said the Commander.

Puff smiled at the magic words, and pressed 'Enter' on his computer keyboard, making the prompt disappear from their screens and a new confirmation appear:

COURSE CORRECTION: APPROVED

The computer screens refreshed and the dotted line that originally showed a highly elliptical trajectory back to Earth switched to a new line that ended at Jupiter.

Hugo Evrard, Ahmed Reygan, Trevor Puffant, Aki Suru, Sophia Iolienne, Olivia Newton and Becky Lange were enroute to Europa.

Chapter 1

Becky Lange was annoyed.

Annoyed with her husband.

He had predicted this would happen.

The *Odyssey* had been barreling through the vastness of interplanetary space for the past three months, and it just hit her. Missing her family. They had already reached a distance from Earth where live communications were no longer possible and they were now relying on delayed transmissions of video messages and email. A delay that just kept growing with the distance between Earth and the *Odyssey*.

The excitement of the mission had started fading since the first day aboard, but it was now official. They were all bored. Most of them, at least. Who knew what the Commander thought. Or Aki. Every mission was like this. The first three months are exciting and it's easy to ignore how much she missed her family. Lange couldn't even imagine how tough it was for her husband. Well at least he still had the kids to look after and be with.

Becky Lange had no one, though. She had the crew, of course, but it wasn't the same kind of family. The evenings were lonely now. She looked forward only to night messages from her husband and then a few minutes of watching reruns of a late-90s TV show.

Missing her family made her stomach get some butterflies. It was difficult sometimes. Lange drowned herself in her work to try and not think about the long walks she could be having, bundled up in her winter clothes and her 64 beanie hat and red scarf, along snowy sidewalks of their neighborhood, holding a warm cup of hot-chocolate. Her other hand would be wrapped around Xavier's arm as they shared the moment together.

She dare not send a message to Xavier telling him he was right. He would most certainly reply by saying something like "of course I was right. I'm pretty smart. I'm sure I would be able to tell if I was wrong."

"Oh NO!" came a shout from the dining room.

Lange left her bedroom compartment to see what the commotion was about.

"What? Are you ok?" she asked Puff.

"No, no I'm not. The Reds just launched for Europa."

He was watching the news on the large flat-screen in the dining room while eating his dinner ration. Lange still found it strange that they received different TV channels aboard a ship that was racing toward Jupiter at tens of thousands of miles per hour. But their crewmate Ahmed had explained that all TV was simply a signal being broadcasted. So as long as the signal was powerful enough, they could receive ESPN (she had rolled her eyes at that news), the History Channel, which never talked about history, MTV, which didn't play any music and a few others. Puff was watching a French channel called France 24, which was covering the launch of another capsule into space destined for a ship that would also take the crew toward Jupiter and its moon Europa.

"We already knew that," groaned Becky Lange. She decided to pour herself a cup of tea and sit at the table to watch the news even though they had received the information in a briefing package sent earlier by ISAF since they had advanced knowledge of the launch.

There was something with watching the television though. It was a way for her to just shut down and not think. Not think about her husband or children. Or their life without her; the fact that she wasn't home to take care of them, or do things with them. Pointless things like share laundry duty or make dinner. Or go for walks, skiing, or even just have a normal fight. Let alone sex. At least she was traveling – pretty far. But even then, she was doing it alone. Xavier had told her long ago that traveling alone was not worth it for him. He had traveled much, but without someone to share it all with, it simply was nothing special. There was no way to relate experiences.

So instead, Lange watched the news that recapped how humanity had gotten to the point of launching another crew toward Jupiter's moon called Europa.

The fact that it had all started with a bluff still made Becky Lange smile.

The Chinese government had leaked a fake memorandum intending to set up a base on Europa. The discoveries from previous exploratory probes, missions from Galileo to Juno, had revealed that the small icy world may harbor life and liquid water oceans. With that in mind, the Chinese and their rising power had clearly intended to use their newfound power and knowledge to fund a trip to the Jovian moon.

The Europeans and Americans refused to allow China be the only one to set up an outpost on the moon, and there was a scientific gain to the operation rather than the pure expenditure of money on national pride like had been accomplished during the Cold War. Exploratory probes over the decades had found that Europa was a tantalizing mystery like Mars had been during the late 1800s. The ice-sheets and geysers erupting from the surface of the Galilean moon had fueled speculation that life was possible beyond the blue space-marble that was Earth.

So Western Europe, North America, Japan and Australia immediately began to build their own interplanetary spacecraft together, the *Odyssey*, along with the spare part infrastructures that always went into government planning. That meant a second ship was built in case something happened to the first. Space agencies had determined that the price tag would go down by building two, and the cost was so high that even with some loss of life because of an accident, the enterprise would have to continue – especially in the race with China.

China had bluffed. But at the revelation moment, the point of no return had already been reached in the exploration program. Billions of euros and dollars had been poured into a massive spacecraft enterprise that had no other purpose than to explore beyond the Earth's neighborhood. So the construction, training and calculations continued.

Investigations and a lot of spying from European and North American intelligence agencies also found out that China was planning to benefit from all the discoveries and were poised to write as many academic papers as quickly as they could to earn all the awards possible. Space agencies were required by law to make all their findings public, and Chinese officials had been planning on this.

Western governments quickly made adjustments to their laws, which stipulated they would hold the information and filter it through the space agencies before allowing them to go public. Science had become nationalistic, infuriating many.

Arguments regarding the symbolism behind the mission threatened the entire project. So much so, a private corporation had started to build its own spacecraft with the help from some well-funded oligarchs, cheap labor and every detail about the research conducted to prepare for the mission being free and open to the public. What type of fuels were needed, the alloys required, computer software, glass materials and mountings, food distribution, water recollection – everything had already been researched by the government-funded preparations. All a corporation had to do was build the thing for a fraction of the cost, and they had hopes of beating the squabbling democracies. After all, a corporation could sell every discovery it made for billions of dollars and only to the highest bidder, regardless of the common good. Pictures could be copyrighted and lifesaving cures could be sold only to those who could afford it.

Some pro-business politicians in the Western governments of course had an interest in favoring a private enterprise. They could earn a cut of the profits. They yelled about the exorbitant cost of a failed government experiment. How weak national leaders had been in believing China was heading for Europa. The best hope for humanity's future was in private enterprise. Only hard-working people paying taxes should have access to the knowledge and discoveries that were paid for by the taxpayers. No one else should have the right to be inspired by the most ambitious mission ever that is too complex for a government to perform, let alone a government associated with other governments of questionable interests (since all other governments were a threat to the way of life). Humans would survive thanks to the benevolence of money-making industries. The politicians used their negative outlook about science to convince their populations they should have a say in every decision made within their government, regardless of how much understanding they truly had. A belief in self-righteousness and the words 'job' and 'trillions' were enough to grind the government congresses to a halt, and with them, the funding for the construction of the ship.

An impassioned speech from a former US president and closed door mediation had helped resolved the problem.

That didn't stop people from still complaining (as they were so good at doing) after the deals were signed. An example just presented itself as the news broadcast displayed the names of the astronauts being launched to space. For the *Odyssey*, astronaut selection was designed to form a unity crew. Again, some people expressed outrage. Bumbling, fumbling but without reasoning.

The crew of the *Odyssey* flew with astronauts of all nationalities. This infuriated some proud nations. Fortunately, their lack of knowledge regarding science meant they could easily be ignored. National pride was what had gotten them into the race in the first place. What had caused the expenditure of billions of dollars, euros and yen. The mission had to represent global cooperation like the International Space Station was the lonely beacon of peaceful cooperation between the two former Cold War powers during the horrifying 2016 American presidential comedy show. A military like efficiency and organization had to be created free from the burdens of national pride. A new entity with the sole purpose of getting to Europa with the resources from a dozen nations. Not a dozen different agencies racing to beat each other and duplicating efforts.

ISAF used to stand for the International Security Assistance Force, and it was a NATO combat mission to Afghanistan during the Terror Wars. It was now the International Space Agency Fleet. A wacko European had come up with the idea – take the acronym of a former alliance meant for war and turn it into a peaceful symbol of unity and harmony. NASA, the ESA, JAXA and all other Western space agencies loved it. The cost of the Europa mission was so astronomical that their budgets for all other research was sucked dry. Until an alternate agency was created to combine all the manned spaceflight programs; the new agency that had to be funded in addition to NASA, the ESA, JAXA etc. while still accomplishing the role of exploration. NASA had become to ISAF what JPL was to NASA.

Lange's phone vibrated. She of course did not have any sort of cell-phone service within the ship and certainly not in between the orbits of two planets (Earth and Mars), but the ship did have Wi-Fi and the network allowed all personal messages to come to the personal devices of each crewmember. So when Lange received a message, it was displayed on all devices that connected to her personal IP on the ship. It allowed personal habits to remain, which was a psychological boost. To prevent alienation so early in the mission was critical to ease the crew into their new lifestyle that was going to be the norm for the next 3 or so years.

Taking her phone (which was really only used as a communications and media tablet), she saw it was a notification that a book one of her friends had written back home was being downloaded onto her digital e-ink book. Resisting the desire to replace real books with a digital device that read like a book, Lange was ultimately forced to accept the Kindle e-reader after ISAF made it clear books were heavy. And heavy meant expensive to lob into space. And it didn't help her that Xavier had sided wholeheartedly with ISAF on this matter. Lange now found herself admiring technology though. A friend on Earth could write a story (or novel) on their computer and then email it to someone's e-reader, formatted and ready to be read like a book, without ever having cables touch either of the devices or a printer ever being used to allow the written word to be read.

Four days later, Becky Lange was again feeling the butterflies in her stomach. The ones that signified she missed her children and her homeworld in general. The connection to Earth was temporarily down because of a malfunction in one of the satellites in orbit around the planet designed to relay messages from the *Odyssey* to Earth. Telemetry wasn't lost, nor were messages with ISAF, since they were on a separate network, but what was known as the morale-line was down. And personal messages were part of morale, which meant she couldn't see videos of her kids or send them anything.

The excitement of the mission was still fresh, so she wasn't too concerned. Lange repeated in her mind that she was on a unique adventure and everyone was thinking it was amazing. She was isolated from the rest of Humanity and lived in a universe that was now completely hostile to all life. It was on the rest of the world to be patient with her communications difficulties, not her: she was the adventure-seeking soul that was venturing into the cold unknown. The fact that she didn't feel like she was missing Xavier often was normal; it was still part of the adaptive phase of settling into her new routine. She still took pleasure in looking outside the small porthole in her room, seeing the stars in the distance yet up close, the different parts of the Human engineered pieces of technology keeping them alive in such a cold, barren environment.

The children would understand. This was the ultimate answer Lange told herself whenever she felt herself missing them. This was the answer thousands of people told themselves when they re-upped their military contracts knowing it would take them far from their families to hostile parts of the world. A world she was leaving behind. With her own family left on it.

With the networks down, the crew was able to look at the video banks that had been uploaded by the world, and Puff was the most enthusiastic to mock different videos. It was like an onboard YouTube. But Lange and the rest of the crew still found it amusing to look at short videos that were intended to be humorous. It broke up the monotony of having to conduct scientific experiments while preparing for the Europa mission while also trying to maintain personal relations on Earth. Experiments which could have been conducted in Low Earth Orbit using the old International Space Station or something like that – but to save money, LEO flights were cancelled and experiments would be conducted by the Europa mission while they transited to the Jovian system.

Chapter 2

"Hey, boss?" called out Ahmed over the ship's PA.

The Commander groaned and got off the treadmill, having specifically left her private radio in her room so that she wouldn't be disturbed while doing her run. But the crew still found a way.... They were like children: you try to get a full night of sleep but the baby still wakes up. And so do you, and you still inexplicably love your children, just like she loved her crew.

"Go?" replied the Commander over the small call box next to the ladder that led to the gym.

"Secure package for your eyes only from ISAF HQ."

"Is it porn?" barged in Puff over the PA.

"I'll be right over," replied the Commander. "And Puff's got cleaning duties tonight. Ahmed, shut off the PA."

"Whaa..." the PA cut off Puff's complaint as Ahmed complied and turned off the system.

The Commander had fortunately only run 0.11 kilometers on the machine, which means she had not been given any time to sweat.

"Sorry Becky," smiled the Commander as she grabbed her bottle. "I'll lift with you another time, but if I were a betting woman, I'd say whatever that message says isn't all that great. You know, since it's super-tip-top-secret and all."

Becky Lange nodded her head in agreement and considered her workout options as the Commander walked to her small bedroom compartment. Lange had been trying to begin a weight lifting routine for the long trip but had found little motivation. The Commander didn't care at all (*at all*) about lifting weights but had agreed to try it with Lange, if only to help her crewmate get a start on a project she had since leaving their homeworld.

Lange sighed, knowing the Commander was right: whenever ISAF logged a message as secret, it meant something was up and the news was to be presented by the Commander of the ship to the crew. That meant that the Commander was most likely going to call a crew meeting soon. So Lange chose instead walk around their home and give everyone the heads up.

A half-hour later, the Commander got to the dining room and was surprised to see everyone was already just waiting there quietly.

"What's up, buttercup?" called out Puff, breaking the tense silence.

"There's news," started the Commander. "Most have you have probably heard of INC?"

"The private consortium that lost the bid for the Europa mission?" asked Olivia for clarification.

"That's the one."

"Didn't another group pay to have the ship built, anyways?" also asked Lange. "The mass production of parts helping make our ship construction cheaper?"

"Who cares?" muttered Puff. "They launched that ship after we launched ours and we boarded the *Odyssey* before their boat came back to Earth following their trajectory set-up."

"Puff is right," added the Commander. "But they went faster," she added, surprising her crew. "Not by much, but ISAF just came down with the calculations, and the information is conclusive. The Indo-Russian consortium ship with current velocities will reach Europa before us. BEFORE," continued the Commander, raising her voice to prevent everyone's reflex to ask questions, "before we concede that they will land on the moon before us, Hugo, I want you and I to run the data points one more time and see what it would take for us to arrive a little earlier than planned and perhaps beat them. We're still far enough out that we can accelerate. ISAF sent me the data but no instructions, so I suspect it'll be up to us to decide."

"No instructions could also mean that there is simply no option," softly added Ahmed.

"I'm not accepting that point, yet. Meet back in the living room in an hour and Hugo will have details for all of us," ordered the Commander.

After the hour passed, the Commander stoically sat on a high chair behind the couches and love-seats the others were sitting in. Hugo had already briefed her the reality of the situation, and they were just waiting on Puff to arrive before continuing.

"Alright, I'm here," said Puff as he jumped onto the couch and rested his feet on the coffee table. The Commander pushed Puff's feet off the table before sitting back down again, allowing Hugo to explain what it would take to accelerate and why all seven of them had all been summoned to the living room.

When Hugo was done explaining, Ahmed simply closed his eyes in realization. Aki remained expressionless, instead opting for a silent, deep breath while staring at the floor of the *Odyssey*. She quietly took the moment to process the dilemma.

Puff though, had his eyebrows raised, showing he would need a bit more explanation from his crewmates to understand what the problem was. Becky Lange was also staring around with big eyes. She knew that some of the crew understood something she didn't, and temporarily cursed her lack of expertise in astrodynamics and engineering before Ahmed sighed a quick explanation.

"Higher velocity would mean we need more fuel."

"You said that."

"More fuel means more weight."

"We've been over this..." groaned Puff, not looking for a recap of basic physics and propulsion.

"What he's saying is that we have to shed weight somewhere else to allow the extra fuel burn," chimed in the normally silent Aki. "Someone has to stay aboard the *Odyssey*."

The realization hit Lange like a brick wall. She no longer sat up straight, but instead hunched over into a deep thinking position. Decades of trials, formal and informal ones; a professional lifetime of work motivated by a child's dreams to reach for the stars had placed the entire crew where they were today. Not in the professional sense of arriving here where they were – it was very much meant in the physical, location, sense. They were placed in the void between the gargantuan Jupiter and the thin asteroid belt within Humanity's home Solar System. Their hopes were all focused on one goal: to walk upon Europa and explore a new world. They would go to bed looking up into the night sky to see the gorgeous Jovian planet as their moon. And someone could be robbed of that opportunity.

"What does ISAF have to say about this?" asked Lange.

"Nothing. They've stayed silent," replied the Commander. "They've got half the PhDs on the planet working for them: someone has already thought of everything we're considering probably, which means Earth is leaving this decision for us to make. ISAF knows there's nothing they can do to stop our decision."

"They could override the propulsion algorithms to prevent us from speeding up."

The Commander conceded that point but then added another perspective of why ISAF wouldn't do it: "accelerating against orders would create more problems to rectify and further endanger the mission since it would require a burn to slow back down. If we chose to accelerate, they would not stop us after the fact. They'd live with it. If we chose not to accelerate and they boosted us, then we could mutiny and have no one agree to go down to the moon until after it's too late."

"So it's up to us," finally said Lange.

"It is. You must decide whether or not to leave someone aboard the *Odyssey* and not land on Europa for national pride," confirmed the Commander.

Lange, wearing her hair down, allowing it to wave lightly just as it grazed her soft shoulders, stared at her warm mug wafting a sweet, lemony smell from her tea. The mug was emblazoned with a cruelly ironic three-letter logo: TBD. To Be Determined. A decision had to be made: prevent someone from walking on Europa, or allow the Indo-Russian corporation to beat them to the Jovian moon and prove global superiority while embarrassing the rest of the world that had supported the mission to bring her this far.

"Not much of a decision, I suppose," replied Lange.

"What do you mean?" asked Puff. "We were clearly handed a decision to make."

"I meant it's an easy one. We stay the course. We can't ask someone to burn their seat off the landing vehicle, the *Columbiad*, for the sake of national pride. This isn't the Space Race anymore."

"Well it would be nice to remind the Russians that they should have joined our team instead of them going their way," mumbled Puff. "But I'll walk to their place when we land on Europa and tell them myself, I suppose. Because this guy is not giving up his seat."

"How selfless of you," grinned the Commander. "There are geopolitical concerns that still need to be considered, but for now, we stay the course and we'll all land on the moon together."

"Um, boss, we're not on Earth. Geopolitics don't apply to Jupiter and its system."

"You are still coming back to Earth, and our actions here have a profound impact on Humanity's future actions in the Universe."

"Of course they do," added Puff as he jumped up. "No one can fix the M-55-A1 like me. I'm kind of a big deal, really the biggest deal." He continued his self-praises as he stepped through the hatch to another compartment. Lange was thankful she didn't have to listen to him anymore.

Ahmed and Hugo both left for the Planning Room to study the trajectory and timeline of the Indo-Russian spacecraft in more detail and Olivia went to prepare some snacks that others could choose to enjoy later. She certainly wasn't going to eat the whole bag of inflatable bread. Meanwhile, Aki decided to float to the cupola of the *Odyssey* for some PR. She was very popular with the East Asian communities and was an adept artist – she had drawn some hilarious manga of the crew aboard the *Odyssey* as well as some gorgeous landscape images of what Europa looked like from the exploratory probes sent ahead of the Human pioneers.

This left Becky Lange and the Commander alone in the Living Room. Becky was still nursing her tea, thinking of the dilemma she had been faced with. She remembered the discussions she had trudged through since her first days in her professional space career: the questions of national pride and flags designating cultures parceled by invisible lines on a planet now too far to even see. Becky reminded herself that the flag wasn't just a symbol of the territorial claims of a state, but of its culture. The hopes and aspirations, philosophies, services and the ideas espoused by such societies were contained inside of those symbols which were the flags. That's why it did matter to her who would land on Europa first. To show the world that the Universe was being explored by a group of Humans that belonged to a community that shared the same values as her.

She shook her head. Regardless of who came first, that wouldn't change. Lange, and the rest of the crew of the *Odyssey* would land and still spread that message. The corporation would be there with them, first or not, to broadcast their own message. Part of her message was to allow anyone to express themselves – even if it meant cringing in respectful silence as someone championed the exact opposite of your own societal beliefs.

"I did not expect having to think about these sorts of decisions when I became an astronaut," admitted Lange as she stared outside the nearest window peering into the inky-blackness of deep-space.

The Commander smirked at the comment, staring at the floor before looking at Becky. "I did," she smiled.

Becky grinned in agreement. She was happy she didn't have to be the unlucky soul in charge of their voracious bunch on a foreign world.

"Do you remember when you found out you were admitted to the Corps?" asked the Commander.

Becky Lange smiled in remembrance.

"I do. Joseph Augustine and Anupama Mukherjee were the ones who knocked on the door. They simply smiled when they handed me the access badge reserved for astronauts with a yellow Post-It on top of it. The Post-It only had a question mark on it."

"That's creative."

"It was. I took off the Post-It note and took the badge. Anu hugged me, Joe shook my hand, and they simply said: 'give us your decision when you're ready. Not now.' Joe was so soft about it. He just gave me a wink. He's a good guy."

"He is," remembered the Commander.

"Xavier had popped open a bottle of champagne the moment the door shut. He had it ready, I guess, knowing I was admitted. I still don't know if he actually knew or if he was just being an optimist. He's always been shady about those things; behind the scenes dealings and decisions. He's somehow always been adept at either being in them or at a minimum, deeply informed about them."

"Well at least you had champagne."

"We did. And then the terror hit," said Lange with a more serious tone. "Adeline came out of her bedroom when she heard the bottle pop."

"Why was that terrifying?"

"Because I realized I had to decide whether or not to leave her on Earth."

The Commander didn't say anything. Attempting to feign sympathy for such a decision was ill-conceived at best, insulting at worst. There was no way to aid in the decision to leave your children on a planet for your own interests in exploring space. This had been a decision for

Becky Lange to make and it was simply morally impossible to judge her decision.

"Well regardless of how you feel about the decision, I'm glad to have you with us aboard. I need someone with your infectious laugh to lighten the mood whenever Puff gets out of hand."

Becky smiled at the compliment. She suddenly realized that the Commander and her, even though all their training and time together aboard the *Odyssey*, rarely ever talked or bonded. They could read the tone of each other's voices, predict each other's movements throughout the mission checklist items, but on a personal level, Becky had never really spoken to her. This was probably one of the first personal compliments the Commander gave her.

"Didn't Xavier specifically refuse a slot of his own for the children and to allow you to launch?" asked the Commander.

"I still don't know if I forgive him for that," admitted Lange. "He didn't tell me he had been admitted. I only found out because someone forgot to shred an old flight roster with his name on it, before he refused a flight position at ISAF."

"I don't know if he's got a better view from where he's from," suggested the Commander.

"What do you mean?"

"He gets a front row seat to see you walk on Europa. I don't think he could have taken a mission had it meant you stay on Earth. There was no way he would forgive himself."

Becky quietly agreed with the Commander.

"Well I suppose we came close to having one of us not make it on the ground anyways."

"Speaking of which," added the Commander as she rose to her feet. "I have to go talk to Mr. Evrard about our newfound race against the Indians and Russians."

Lange nodded her head as the Commander left the living room, leaving her in isolation to observe the cosmos. Peering into the vastness of space, Becky knew that the enormous expanse of the Universe paled in size compared to the depth of her own mind and imagination. Lange decided to imagine being at home, with her husband and children. She smiled remembering the pathetic, cheesy love lines Xavier would tell her. She tried to imagine what kind of ridiculous, eye-rolling line he would say to her right now as she was a little down from the news that they would arrive second on Europa, but couldn't come up with anything. She could only smile and shake her head at the memories of their past.

Lange pulled out her cell-phone and started to record a quick hello to her family. It was quick and almost a little emotionless. Becky Lange didn't want to allow the floodgates of emotions to open at this moment. She was so far from home that there was no way for her to speak to anyone live, other than her fellow crewmates. The message was recorded and channeled through the digital systems of the *Odyssey* before the ship fired a laser toward what looked like empty space.

Just over 51 minutes later, a satellite in orbit around the Earth received those faint laser-light pulses and retransmitted them back to Earth for Lange's family to watch.

Chapter 3

A 90s-era music beat resonated through Lange's private compartment, her morning song from the band Sum 41 announcing the start of a new day according to the human biological clock. As far as the *Odyssey* was concerned, it was day all the time. There was no point in trying to cycle anything to the Earth or Europan 'days'. Given that their destination was tidally locked with Jupiter and it took the moon 3.5 days to run a lap around the gas giant, defining day and night according to the light from the sky would be a tough proposition at best; even if there was no illumination from the Sun, Jupiter still would be reflecting a good deal of light back. So the astronauts were living according to a 24 hour day based on a clock called Zulu – the universal time of Earth. Which would soon become Europa's universal time as well.

But this was not what Lange cared about this early in the morning. She turned on her laptop and saw that there was an email from home. She leaned over her bunk to reach for the light-switch next to her door (it was within arm's length inside the tiny personal room allocated to her) and turned it on before activating the record button on the small personal webcam near her.

When she was satisfied she was recording, Becky Lange opened the email from Mr. and Children Lange. There was a note and video recording. Reading the note, the webcam recorded the smiles and smirks Lange revealed. She laughed out loud when watching the video sent to her. Recording the eye-rolls Becky was executing with a beaming smile, the webcam chronicled all of her reactions. At one moment, her husband and 3 year old looked at each other with blank stares after being asked a question – the two men she cared for the most in the Universe were just *so* adorable. Even in his adult age, her husband was able to act like a baby with their baby. When the video reached its end, Becky looked at her webcam and said a quick hello.

"Hi everyone. Thank you for the email. I thought it was funny. I've got to head to the lab but I'll send you guys a message later."

As she shut off her webcam, the computer automatically sent back home the recording of her reaction to the video and email. It allowed her family to feel close to her and informed them on what made her laugh. Seeing Lange's expressions and emotions as she read her messages or watched videos, even though she was so far away, helped maintain their relationship.

A relationship that the mission planners considered making officially non-existent. Initial proposals suggested making a voyage to Europa a 'for celibates only' enterprise. When Xavier found out ISAF was considering making it a singles only trip, he had promptly filed for divorce along with other ISAF members that thought that the families would be capable of taking decisions themselves. Combined with public pressure from Western nations to allow people who declared love to be allowed to travel to the stars, ISAF relented, even if the mission was to last 3 years.

Lange sighed. *Three years.* At least almost one was complete, so she was almost a third of the way through the voyage... Almost. Lange and the rest of the crew preferred to round up and tell themselves that they would arrive soon.

In two years, she would set foot back on Humanity's homeworld. In between, though, she would be walking upon Europa, and in a sense, as she walked aboard the *Odyssey*, she could be considered walking between Earth and the Jovian system. That's probably enough to silence those proud marathoners who liked to show-off their preparative exercises to make Becky feel like she wasn't the most physically fit in the world.

Passing through the kitchen to get herself a ration and some water, Becky Lange then rejoined her pet plants that she was responsible for.

The long voyage meant that spacelifting tons and tons of food for the crew to survive on was inefficient. The plants Lange took care of had multiple benefits: they fed Humans, which was a pretty big deal, but they also helped in the recirculation of air and oxygen, which was an even bigger deal. Lange still loved them for the simple, natural, innate sensation. The plants were a small piece of greenery in an otherwise obscure, empty expanse. Lange had managed to grow a few extra plants without dipping into the resources of the ship too much, so to the surprise (or complete ignorance) of her fellow crewmates, plants were popping up in random rooms, between the Living Room, the Kitchen and even a small bonsai on the Flight Deck. She kept one on her window sill; Lange may not be permitted to bring her pet dogs or children with her, but she would at least have her plants.

So Becky continued to tend to her plants through the morning. Water levels and consumption for the *Odyssey* were calculated, output of the plants as well, power-consumption for the lamps sustaining life aboard the vessel. What were the engineers on Earth doing? Lange knew they were triple checking her work. And she was working to keep busy. Otherwise, the trip time would get very boring, very quickly. And she preferred to be informed about what was happening with her biological lab anyways. She was the primary biologist for the mission, after all.

A few hours later, Lange stopped her centrifuge from spinning. She thought she had heard some...

There it was again!

A whisper.

She frowned in confusion.

The chilling murmur sounded again.

She suddenly relaxed. Lange had heard this whisper before. And it was calling for Becky.

"What do you want, Puff?" she called out loud.

"Hey! I've got to go outside to take a look at the outflow pump valve on number 4. Can you spot me?" he said popping his head into Lange's lab.

She took a deep breath but agreed.

"Yeah. I need a break anyways. How long is it going to take for you to get dressed?"

"I don't know. Before getting dressed I have to get undressed: how long is it going to take for you to take my clothes off?"

"I'm going to get a snack in the kitchen and I'll meet you at the airlock," replied Lange, having learned long ago to ignore Puff's advances.

"Sounds good. Airlock two, by the way."

How Puff had gotten a clean bill of health from the ISAF psychologists, sociologists and psychiatrists was beyond Becky Lange. He probably was a really good engineer. And he made her laugh most of the time through his groaning.

Ten minutes later, the two were at the aft airlock of the ship, Puff all suited up for his Extra-Vehicular Activity, or within their acronym repertoire: EVA. Becky certainly went WTF when she saw the acronym dictionary for this mission. When they started training, she was convinced there was no way she'd ever get it all straight. She was wrong.

"Is your O_2 RV activated?" she asked Puff as she continued checking his equipment over.

"It is now," replied Puff as he finished latching a hose and pressed a switch.

With her final checks complete, Lang went into a full litany of confirmations with Puff using a decidedly professional and neutral tone.

"EP is green, good seal on 1, 2, 3 and 4, AMJ link is green, we'll check also in the lock...9 is good, ADTJ in AUTO, VMRE fully loaded. You're good to go."

"Oh no," said Puff with a sudden air of concern.

"What?"

"I need to use the bathroom..."

Lange rolled her eyes with a smile and shoved the glass, domed helmet to Puff.

"Call me when you're sealed and inside the lock," she said as she floated up the tunnel to the Flight Deck.

It took her an actual full minute to get there given the length of the ship; the airlock and the Flight Deck were located the very opposite ends of the ship.

Ballistically entering the flight deck, Lange flipped over and landed on the metal plate located opposite the tunnel exit. Engineers were angry with the astronaut's request to put the metal plate there; it was solely so that they could travel faster through the ship and use it as a landing pad, instead of just slowly rising of the tunnel and not crash into the walls of the ship – engineers and construction workers couldn't understand why the astronauts insisted that they be able to just go as fast as possible through their spacecraft that sustained their lives. Astronauts argued that they were going to be in that spaceship for 2 years and would make the changes themselves if they had to, which could be ill-implemented and increase the risk to the mission.

The astronauts won the argument.

Hugo and the Commander were already in the flight deck. They had been spending more time together, Lange noted, but she soon brushed it off as normal. They were approaching the Jovian system which was a critical time for the ship's navigator and the Commander.

"Hey, Becky," said the Commander noticing Lange arriving. "What brings you to the head of the ship?"

"Puff is going for a walk," smiled Lange as she took her seat at the EVA monitoring consol.

"Awesome. Are you his spotter?"

"Yeah. He's in airlock 2 and I already signed him off."

"Great. Let me know if you need help or you want me to take over. I'll be here, anyways."

"I'm going to take this as a break from the lab for a bit. Plants are exciting... No. No they're not."

The Commander and Hugo laughed.

"What are you guys up to?" continued Becky Lange.

"It looks like we just went into a communications blackout with Earth," explained the Commander. "They're still receiving us but we lost our uplink about twenty minutes ago. No big deal. It happened two weeks ago."

"Yeah," added Hugo. "Ahmed is probably trying to watch Netflix again."

The three of them chuckled at the thought.

"Lt. Uhura, this is Iron Man, ready for the lock to be opened," called Puff over the radio. "I have a good radio, by the way."

"You got it, Puff."

"No, Becky, I'm Iron Man. I'm wearing a suit that can withstand almost anything in this environment. It's even got red stripes."

Lange didn't listen and instead accessed the menu that had the airlock door switch on it and activated it.

From inside the lock, Puff saw the door gape open. Floating and immobile, staring into the emptiness of the Universe, Puff felt like he was standing on the edge of a precipice. An infinite precipice. It was hard to grasp. He could jump out into the dark, glittering canvas in front of him and for millennia, never stop.

Or get sucked toward Jupiter and crash into it because of the gas giant's gravity well.

Maneuvering onto the side of the *Odyssey*, Puff took a good look at the ship they had spent so much time inside, but had decidedly rarely seen the outside of. He and Olivia had often caressed the side of their vessel during space walks, caring for her as she shielded the fragile, squishy human bodies inside from the harshness of deep space; radiation storms, cosmic winds, vacuum.

Puff returned to the task at hand and went to inspect the engines he had grown to know so well (because he had pretty much designed them).

"Becky? You want to grab some food?" called Olivia over the inter-ship radio.

"No I just had a snack. I'm babysitting Puff. He's outside."

"Oh don't let him come back in yet, I need him to check something. I'll be there in a sec."

"Understood... Puff?"

"Iron Man, here."

"Olivia is about to get on the phone, she'll want you to check something out."

"Oh ok, let me drop everything I'm doing to focus on her stuff."

Minutes later, Olivia and her supernova-bright hair arrived.

Lange allowed Olivia to talk to Puff in their engineer speak and Puff agreed to check things out.

"Alright. I'm still famished," said Olivia, when she was done with the radio communication. "Where's Aki?"

Lange looked around and sarcastically answered: "Um... not here."

"Fine. I'm out!" and Olivia floated down the tunnel back to the rotation section of the ship where she would stand and make a meal.

Chapter 4

Hugo and Puff were floating together down the long neck of the *Odyssey* to the flight deck after having been summoned by their Commander to come forth for a briefing regarding communications with Earth.

"Hopefully it's all better now. Mo betta', you know?" said Puff.

"Hopefully," agreed Hugo.

"Whatever caused this communications blackout, I blame Becky," sarcastically poked Puff as he floated up the tunnel to arrive in the Flight Deck.

"If I were to shut any communications off, it would be your ability to communicate, not Earth's," smirked Lange as floated above her seat in her Delta Air Lines hoody and dinosaur pajama shorts.

"Children, behave," said the Commander as she closed a small notification that popped up on one of the screens.

"Where's Aki?" asked Hugo.

On cue, Aki Suru's head popped out of the tunnel leading into the spacecraft. After taking a look at who was already here, Aki noticed she was the last one and floated in a graceful front flip to her seat.

For the past two days, communications from Earth stopped flowing in. Becky Lange had started to tap into her backup video recordings from her family to keep following her daily tradition of getting a message from them. Fortunately, the *Odyssey* was still broadcasting loudly back to the planet and got the automated confirmation soft pings saying Earth was receiving them. But why they weren't receiving anything else from Earth was a bit of a mystery. One that hopefully would be revealed now.

"Alright, guys," sighed the Commander. "I'll start by saying the communications blackout is no longer an issue and you have personal messages downloading to your inboxes right now. However, there are a few things we need to talk about first."

The crew's mood became somber. The Flight Deck was always kept dark and bathed in a soft red hue, which only amplified the serious ambiance.

"First," started the Commander, "we have accelerated. We're not accelerating to a point where we will beat the Russians and Indians, but where we will be arriving at the same time as them. Additionally, we've adjusted the trajectory and we'll be heading to the tertiary landing site... Let me finish, Puff. The reasons are simply this: someone has taken the Earth hostage."

The crew's reaction resembled that of surprised pigeons; their heads cocked back and eyes blinked all at the same time. The Commander would have found it funny had the circumstances been different.

"The backup spacecraft modules, propulsion, living etcetera launched for this mission have been diverted by a clever man by the name of Doctor Julien Montsegur. He has managed to latch onto to a small asteroid and get it locked and aimed at Earth. That's the extreme, Fox-News simplistic and dumbed down to Republican stupidity version of the situation. His demands are simple: world unity. He wants to see serious efforts to unifying the planet and mutual assistance for each other. If not, he will release the rock and hope the global cataclysm will hit the reset button on Humanity, similar to how the World Wars changed the world order. If anyone from Earth tries to intercept him or launch spacecraft, he bombs Earth. ISAF can provide you with more details if they agree. This is still a secret. Dr. Montsegur has contacted only heads of states and has not made any of this public. It's probably on a matter of time before a leak in one of our democratic nations reveals it globally, but for now, you are some of the few Humans in the Universe who know about this."

"Who the hell is this guy?" asked Olivia.

"An idealist," said the Commander flatly.

Without additional information provided, Hugo continued to prod.

"Ok... How did he get to space and commandeer a ship to then grab an asteroid? Isn't that piracy – taking a ship without permission?"

"He had permission because it was his. Asteroid capture isn't difficult, and neither is building a rocket. The obstacle to those things is cost. Dr. Montsegur received a lot of support by presenting himself as a rich man trying to be the first solo astronaut to fund his own flight to space. Through shell companies, he also received funding for the spacecraft that would take the asteroid. The cost was relatively low thanks to the insane costs associated with building the *Odyssey* and its backup ship currently headed to Europa. The space agencies had used a well-known government purchase idea called COTS: Commercial Off The Shelf. Many of the spacecraft parts and compartments had already been built for ISAF and others, so that kept the prices low in some areas. In other areas, Dr. Montsegur was able to acquire parts of the ships that had been left behind on Earth, either because they weren't useful or they would have added too much weight – various reasons. He would have a use for them though.

"When Dr. Montsegur launched on his mini-spacecraft to show the solo-spaceman act, he docked with the larger project that had been funded by hedge-funds and built using left-over parts. The rest is what you know: he captured the rock, aimed it at Earth. An Intel brief will be provided by ISAF soon. Dr. Augustine suggested that Dr. Montsegur saw some stuff in the third world that hit him hard. He's former US military and saw multiple deployments, and apparently lost some family or close people. Who knows what drove him to do this. The important part is that he did. All communications from Earth to him are cut, and any launches from Earth detected, will be seen as an attempt to disarm him, which means he'll release the rock."

"He must have a hell of a pair of eyeballs to be able to see launches from Earth," grumbled Puff.

"Dr. Montsegur has sensors in orbit around the Earth similar to the SBIRS constellation belonging to the US. It can sense any launch on Earth using infrared and ultraviolet sensors detecting the heat plume from a launch system. He also claims to have several radars pointed toward the Earth fencing him off from any satellite that would be rammed against him."

"Food? Water?" asked Lange.

"He has enough to last him for seven hundred days."

"That takes him almost to the time when we're supposed to get home."

"That's no coincidence."

"When is it ever?" muttered Puff.

"Dr. Montsegur's ultimatum has a deadline," continued the Commander. "If by the time the missions to Europa are scheduled to return planetary reforms haven't been started, then he'll release the rock. He hasn't really asked for anything else."

"So is this why we're accelerating? To begin this unification process?" asked Lange.

"We're going to show unity by landing with the Russians?" asked Puff, not caring to wait anymore.

"Partially," answered the Commander. "The acceleration and course change still cost us in fuel, and the original concern of having to leave someone behind aboard the *Odyssey* has not changed." The Commander looked at her crew before revealing who was chosen to not land on the moon. "I will stay aboard the *Odyssey*".

This time, everyone frowned and they were all about to start talking before the Commander continued.

"This is not worth arguing about, so keep quiet. I came up with this simple plan, and so far I believe it will work. ISAF is considering it, but even if they don't, I will execute it unless they can provide a proper reason not to. This can and will most likely be considered mutiny if they disagree, which is why I have not kept any of you in the loop except for Hugo. Hugo will be taking command and I needed his expertise for the orbital calculations. I will take the *Odyssey* on an accelerated path around the Jovian system back toward Earth, which is why we had to adjust course."

"Wow, hold on," interrupted Puff. "You're taking the *Odyssey* on an accelerated path back to Earth?"

"How will we return to Earth?" asked Aki.

"You will be landing at site 3 on Europa, which is only two kilometers from the Russian landing site. They didn't bother to do research on where to land and instead stole our plans and landing site research. They also didn't expect us to land there, so they thought their experiments could still be unique. Once on the ground, you will run your experiments as quickly as you can. Becky and Olivia, I need you to start condensing the biological and geological experiment timeline as much as you can."

"Condense them? By how much?" asked Lange.

"Your one year is down to three months."

"Three months?" exclaimed the entire crew.

"That's how long it will take the *Otkrytiye* to..."

"I'm sorry, the Ot- what?" interrupted Puff.

"Ote-kree-tee," slowly explained the Commander. "It's the Russian mothership. It means Discovery."

"We're calling it Discovery then," gabbled Puff.

"The *Otkrytiye*," continued the Commander, ignoring Puff's recommendation, "will take three months to slingshot around Jupiter before swinging back to Europa to pick you up."

"If ISAF doesn't know about this until now, how do you know that the Indians and Russians will pick us up?"

"Because I've been talking to the *Otkrytiye*." The shocking news just kept coming! Lange was wondering how many shoes could keep dropping. "Since ISAF didn't allow communications with us anyways, I decided to move the communication dishes on our spacecraft to talk to Russians and Indians. We're close enough that discussions now are virtually instantaneous. Virtually. The *Otkrytiye* will pick you up three months after the landing, and you'll head back to Earth with them. Puff, you and Hugo will need to work together to see how much food you can keep for your return trip while still being able to lift-off from Europa. Right now the plan is for you to live in the *Columbiad* even after docking with *Otkrytiye*. They obviously didn't plan on taking six more astronauts so they don't have living quarters. Fortunately, since the *Columbiad* was rated to stay for over a year on Europa, the return trip to Earth will count toward that time given how short the stay on Europa will be. It *will* sustain you. The *Otkrytiye* has two extra docking ports: you'll take one of them as your parking spot. So that's the bottom line:

you will land, united with the Russians and Indians, explore the world together for 3 months, using your unity of efforts to accomplish more work in less time. Three months later, you will lift off from Europa, dock with the *Otkrytiye*, and head back to Earth to be reunited with your loved ones."

The crew took a collective deep breath. The quiet ship continued to whir and randomly beep around them, the lights loyally bathing the cockpit continuously, completely unaware of the Human problems being discussed within its hull. The astronauts were still processing the information. Lange had unconsciously started to condense into a little ball upon herself, pulling her sleeves over her hands, snuggling inside of something familiar and comfortable; a feeling that was desperately in short supply right now. They simply had to go through the mindset logically: the only thing that had *really* changed was the timeline. They were going to spend less time on Europa. But that contingency had already been considered during the long months prior to the mission ever launching. In case something came up while off-world, they would just rocket back into space and away from what was potentially a dangerous world. So all the Commander told them was happening was a shorter timeline, a different home, which was always nice (the *Odyssey* would have gotten boring anyways, probably), and the Commander wasn't going. Lange kicked herself for having put that aside of her mind up to now.

"Wait a minute: that's what we're doing," said Lange. "What about you?" she asked the Commander.

"I will ram the *Odyssey* into Dr. Montsegur's ship and the asteroid he is docked to. Like you guys said: the Cold War is over. No one can hold our planet hostage anymore. On this, we are all united in agreement. And that should be enough for Dr. Montsegur."

"You're going to ram him?" asked Puff. "Like crash into him? Can I come?"

The crew chuckled.

"Won't he release the asteroid?" asked a concerned Lange.

"The change in trajectory we're taking right now will put the *Odyssey* in an out-of-plane trajectory."

"She'll be coming from above," clarified Hugo. "So even if Dr. Montsegur is looking over his shoulder instead of Earth, which is where we suspect he's truly focused on, he won't see the Commander arriving from above. By the time they impact, there won't be a chance for Montsegur to accelerate the asteroid enough."

"*Doctor* Montsegur," corrected the Commander. "Besides, he doesn't know that we're changing the plan and that I'll be arriving a full year ahead of schedule. As far as he's concerned, we're too far to do anything about this. Earth will proceed with his unification process for the next year, because it's not a *bad* idea, but the planet will regain its right to choose in a year or so when the *Odyssey* returns home."

The rest of the crew started to realize that this was going to be a one way trip for the Commander. She couldn't let them get all emotional right now. They needed to start thinking and planning for contingencies that were being briefed.

"So we're accelerating toward Europa, meaning we can't all fit on the *Columbiad*," recapped Puff. "Once we land, you," he pointed to the Commander, "will continue with the *Odyssey*, since you can't fit aboard the *Columbiad*..."

"And someone should be aboard to effect repairs for the return voyage."

"Not true, my engine is perfect, but you will take the *Odyssey* back to Earth to destroy the threat. And we're all going to go home holding hands with Russians and Indians. Did I get that right?"

"That's right. Now, that's everything. Get going. Not of word of this to your families, yet. Becky, biology and squishy living things, Puff, engine requirements, Aki, power supplies for the *Columbiad*, Ahmed, supplies and Olivia, geological timeline constraints and systems we can leave on Europa for future observations or explorers. Go."

The astronauts started to float out of their spots toward the tunnel, silently. The mood aboard the ship wasn't for socializing right now. Even so far from Earth, its issues continued to affect them.

The familiar beep that signified a message from ISAF rung through the Flight Deck and the crew hovered over the tunnel as the Commander displayed it on one of the large screens.

Still considering it all. In meantime, only spouses authorized situation update.
202911081002Z//NC//1900Z

"Talk about unity," muttered the Commander. "Dr. Montsegur would be ecstatic ISAF can't make up its mind about this. You can tell your families. Get out."

The crew floated down the tunnel before spreading across the ship to find a spot to send a message home.

Chapter 5

Lange was having trouble realizing that they were now accelerating through space again. She didn't know how she felt about this. She couldn't tell if she was disappointed by the shortened time on Europa she would be allowed, or if the Commander sacrificing her seat for the extra fuel, or the idea of living with the Russians and Indians for a year, or perhaps the obvious morale conundrum that the Commander now knew she was going to kill herself in one year.

Sitting on her bed, she tried to sort through her emotions before recording a message for Xavier to explain to him the situation. As far as he knew, she had told him a joke about what had happened last night at dinner with Hugo and Puff, which meant things were just perfect aboard the *Odyssey*.

"Hey boss, why was there a communications blackout by the way? We could talk to Earth but not Earth to us?"

"ISAF didn't want to risk having you guys find out from Earth the hostage situation before they briefed it to us."

"So how did you work on the plan with the Russians and Indians?"

"ISAF hadn't warned me about the blackout. I suppose it was just a shut it down first, sort it out later mindset. Don't forget that they were probably the first to find out since they own all the communications sites around the planet that Dr. Montsegur is using to broadcast to Earth."

"That's true," sighed Lange.

"So with the blackout, I thought I would see what our options were to fix it in case it was an actual severe problem. You guys were all sleeping because they cut comms during our sleep hours. But I was up, so I tried to communicate with the *Otkrytiye* in case we wanted to use them as a relay. I hadn't figured out how to broadcast it yet, but the next day when I woke up, I got the explanation from ISAF and then I started talking to *Otkrytiye* to figure out what options we could come up with. You were then brought into the loop. I recorded a message every two hours to ISAF asking them to lift the information blackout from you."

"Two hours?" replied Olivia. "Blimey, you should have been sending a message every minute! Every second! You should have bloody told us, is what you should have done."

"Yeah, what's up with that..." started Ahmed before being interrupted.

"Enough," said the Commander. "You know just as well as I do that I couldn't disregard ISAF's instructions regarding this."

"Blood or not," continued Puff, "we're looking at beating the Russians to Europa now. I need to come up with some solid zingers for the Russian guy who thinks he knows how his engines work."

"Be nice, Puff. Like you just said: they're his engines. Not yours."

"Hey I designed some of it."

"Yes, but how would you feel if he came aboard and tried to tell you how to run your engines."

"He wouldn't..."

"Puff..."

"He wouldn't because he'd be *wrong*! I know everything about those machines. Since I know everything, he can't teach me anything. Bad example, Commander."

The Commander smirked. Puff was going to be in for a rough surprise. Looking at Hugo, he was also smiling and shaking his head silently. He also knew the surprise and the Commander was confident that the surprise would stay a surprise until they got aboard the *Otkrytiye*.

The venting to the Commander was short-lived.

It didn't really help with Becky's frustrations, though. The news wasn't good, and she felt like ISAF had abandoned her. Well, not really. ISAF was doing what it could do. It was the Commander that was doing all the decision making the dark. Yes, she was the Commander, but it didn't change the fact that they were a crew aboard an interplanetary starship.

The scientist and astronaut couldn't help but feel that others were being favored. Hugo of all. The Commander had gone to him for different calculations. Yes, Hugo was a fine navigator, but Becky Lange still could be useful in the decision making process. She was a decorated military officer with valuable insight. Why couldn't the Commander see that?

She sighed thinking about how she was treated compared to others. Even Puff had free-reign to do whatever he wanted. The ship engineer was the brains of the whole operation given his knowledge of the primary propulsion systems.

Aki was remarkably silent and zen. It was so relaxing. Becky only wished she actually showed emotions sometimes. Or at least knew how Aki kept her cool all the time. There had to be something that Aki felt strongly about? Or how did she actually not care about anything? Maybe it was because Aki was always so nice she was already highly viewed by everyone. And she didn't work for ISAF permanently – the

Japanese astronaut was accomplishing this one mission and then it was done for her, probably. She didn't have the same 'career-progression' baggage that Becky and other members of the crew had to deal with. Then again, Becky didn't really need to worry about her career either. She was travelling to Europa!

She shook her head. Becky knew what frustrated her was not the career aspects of it, but it was instead the fact that she sometimes felt like the crew didn't respect her enough to ask her for contributions.

It was probably all in her head. Lange knew that the frustrations were due to cabin fever. It was part of the problem of being stuck with the same people for months on end, without relief. The space agencies had already identified these problems in the past and that's why Becky Lange was even able to recognize that.

It didn't matter. She still sometimes felt frustrated with all this.

"Becky?" said the Commander.

"Yes?"

"Well done on the compressed timeline schedule for the surface experiments," smiled the Commander. "I already told the *Otkrytiye* that you were probably going to be the most help on the surface and during the return trip home."

"Thank you," politely smiled Lange.

"I'm going to go talk to Aki now to see if she can make some changes to her plans," grinned the Commander before leaving the room.

Lange was feeling good again. Suddenly.

She knew it was irrational. These mood swings.

She went from rage to joy in just a few seconds. Lange was taught – briefed and even taught again that this was going to happen. Traveling in an environment where natural sunlight would be at a premium, the schedules would be messed up and the close confinement of personnel would mean that there would be mood swings. Frustrated to happy to frustrated. Tomorrow she would again wake up happy. The next day she just wouldn't want to wake up.

The worse part was that there were very few options for her or her crew-mates to get better. They were all going to go through this phase at some point probably. Pride would ensure that no one ever admitted it.

No one on Earth could help. Xavier couldn't really understand, and she didn't want him to. She didn't need him to quietly listen to the irrational frustrations that existed through the poor leadership Becky was seeing. It would probably annoy her to tell him anyways – it was a good thing communications between Earth and the *Odyssey* were no longer instantaneous. With all these frustrations, better not to talk to anyone. *Just leave me be*, is what she wished.

Becky Lange took deep breaths occasionally, knowing that her mood-swings had just started.

There hadn't been any real time for the Commander to adapt yet. Lange had to give her some time. A few weeks. Maybe more, *come on Becky*. Yes. More time before Lange would explode in frustration. That would show whether or not the Commander could listen.

Sometimes, some leaders would learn from the concerns of their subordinates. That was a sign of leadership – that's what set leaders above managers. Anyone with authority could tell someone else to do something. It took a leader to listen to them and let them decide to do that thing.

It's only been a few days since the news dropped, Becky kept telling herself.

Down the corridor, in his own quarters, Ahmed was talking to Olivia. He was venting the same frustrations.

"I fully agree," said Olivia.

"Let's just let a few people decide everyone else's fate," grumbled Ahmed.

"I admit I totally lived through that. You know this is the darkness messing with you," smiled Olivia.

"Yes!" sighed Ahmed. "I know. But you have to admit the Commander is often wasting our time with random taskers and then this compulsion to do team physical training."

"I agree. I'm on the fitness protection program for a reason."

"It was funny the first time," noted Ahmed. "Not the 800 times you've said it since. Pass me a biscuit."

"I can see you are frustrated a bit," replied a sarcastic Olivia. "How about you just watch some comedy show or something and we'll re-attack this later."

"You're right. Thanks."

Olivia left just as Ahmed's phone ringed. He had just received a message from his girlfriend on Earth.

Ugh.

He didn't want to deal with her right now. Ahmed didn't even know how he felt about his relationship. It had been going on for a while before they launched for Europa. But distance had a way of just changing his perspective about things.

The astronaut was also feeling sidelined and disfavored by the Commander. The feeling of uselessness in such an isolated world as the one they were in was difficult. In the grand scheme of things, he was fully aware of the significance of his work and his 'self-worth'. Right now it was difficult to get over it. The mind was a b*** like that.

He looked at the message from his girlfriend:

> I'm having a lovely morning. I've got Frank Sinatra on, and I'm dancing around the kitchen as I attempt to make an omelet for breakfast. I wish you were here.

It was completely harmless, yet it frustrated him. It was completely illogical, he knew it. But it was this kind of message from his girlfriend that would sometimes drive him to think the relationship should just end. After all, if it made him feel that way, doesn't it mean something? Ahmed didn't do anything though because he knew that it could all be his mind messing with him. The long voyage to Europa was going to mess with his mind. With his perception of things.

Because he knew it, he was just going to ignore it for now. A response would be typed out later, when he was in a better mood. Ahmed knew that personal relationships were tough, especially long distance. If she was willing to wait for him this long, then any decision about their relationship could take place when he was back on Earth. Patience was the name of the game.

But his patience with the way things were running on this ship was running out.

The Commander knew that this was happening with Becky Lange (and Ahmed Reygan) and would continue to happen throughout their mission, occasionally. She fortunately recognized it and worked to pull aside the individuals going through these phases. The Commander already made a mental note to pull aside both Becky and Ahmed separately to tell them how valuable they were to the team. She would tell them how critical they would continue to be especially as Hugo would prepare for command.

That reminded the Commander of another duty to perform: she had to prepare her successor. Since she would be taking the *Odyssey* alone, she had to prepare the next leader to command the team on their exploration of Europa and their return trip to Earth.

Chapter 6

Hugo met up with the Commander again and they went over the calculations and orbital plans like they had been doing in secret up to now. They no longer feared being caught by the crew; then again, they had been able to hide in plain sight. People saw them work together, but no one had ever known what they were working on. After all, there was no reason for the crew to suspect any of this in the first place. No one but Hugo cared about the trajectory. Hugo and the rest of the engineers and mission leaders back on Earth. But the Commander still took these moments to try and mentor Hugo who would soon be in charge of some of the brightest Humans that had been on Earth.

"Tensions are going to skyrocket when you guys get aboard the *Otkrytiye*, Hugo."

"What do you mean?"

"We've been living together for the past year. Hell, longer than that when you consider the training portion. Which means you will instantly be more comfortable with the crew you know than the one you don't. You will not approve of the way they do some things, be it their simple customs on how to eat a meal or the way they purge fuel lines. You will all coalesce into your ISAF team that we are, and isolate yourselves from the Indians and Russians. You cannot allow that to happen. Force Puff to work with his counterpart. Lean on Lange: she's your best hope for unification."

"Becky Lange?"

"Any other Langes in this part of the Solar System?"

"Fine. Why her?"

"Do you remember our first few days in the training program?"

"Oh yeah – she was all about making a team name and doing team chants and patches."

"Use her desire for social connections. She's an extrovert, but a benevolent one. Puff is also an extrovert, but not so benevolent. Aki and Olivia will be fine: they're introverts and will have no issue sticking to business as usual with their counterparts."

"That leaves Ahmed. So no problems."

"Ahmed is no problem. He's next in line after you for command and ISAF considered giving him command of a future deep space mission instead of Europa. He is one of the best astronauts we have – better than either you or me."

"Ok... But...?"

"He's Muslim."

"There it is. Hold on: let me get the microphone so you can blare that in the same concerned tone to the rest of the ship."

"I need you to remember that Hindus and Muslims have had deep rooted tensions between each other for a *long* time..."

"You don't think they'll be professionals and nice to each other?"

"You'll soon learn that as the leader your job is not to hope for the best: it's to be ready for the worse... really, you need to be ready for anything. You can't plan for everything, you can only have an awareness. Your crew will make your life easy and I certainly have no doubt that Ahmed and the Indians will have no problems. Especially because Ahmed is a pretty lovable guy. However, if something were to happen and tensions will invariably flare up, you need to ensure it doesn't get into a bigoted contest of whose religion or creed is better. Also," insisted the Commander before Hugo could interrupt her.

"Remember that whatever happens on that ship will affect relations on Earth. Not necessarily between nations, but between peoples. Pride is a plague that has allowed our nations and religions to claim supremacy over each other and our mission of unity needs to display the opposite of that: not division."

"Then on that note, do you know what the crew composition is for the Indians?"

"Two Indians and four Russians."

"I meant gender-wise."

"Two females and four males."

"And we're going to introduce two new females to them."

"Now you're catching on. Again, if they know Lange, they won't even risk a knife fight with her."

"She brought a knife aboard? Isn't that illegal?" asked an incredulous Hugo.

"It was in her private item box that we were all permitted. She did the responsible thing and declared it to me before the launch, and I said it was ok. Olivia has a box of matches – fire hazard but permitted nonetheless, and you as Commander will soon have a nail gun."

"A nail gun?"

"Provided by ISAF for emergency repairs aboard the *Odyssey*, but it obviously could be used as a weapon."

"Ok. Are you sure you don't want to stay? I can take the *Odyssey* and just not worry about matches, knives or nail guns."

The Commander laughed.

Their conversation was interrupted by a SPHERE (Synchronized Position Hold, Engage, Reorient, Experimental) robot that floated next to Hugo with a red blinking light. The purple, dodgeball sized sphere that used small puffs of compressed air to navigate itself in the weightless corridors of the *Odyssey* had a small white name stenciled onto its equatorial line: Leonardo.

"Oh. Looks like Leo can't fix the electrical load bearing in BMAG-number 2."

"The one we were trying to warm up?"

"That's the one."

"What's the word on the thing potentially short-circuiting?"

"Slim to none. I'll still go check it out. It could be a problem with this little guy, too," added Hugo, nodding to the SPHERE.

"Alright. We're done anyways. See you at dinner."

"Adios."

Hugo dove down into the tunnel away from the Flight Deck, the Leonardo robot chasing after him as they headed toward the back of the ship to fix an electrical anomaly. Again.

"Olivia? It's Hugo. I'm headed to the corridor to work on BMAG number 2. Can you help me out with the diagnosis?"

Olivia was hanging out with Lange in the hydroponics lab when she answered: "Oh I'm on my way. That problem ends today. TODAY!"

Lange was working on the plants in the ship and trying to think through the requirements of the Europa research being cut down to only 3 months before the slowdown and right now she was just trying to not get too nauseous walking around the spacecraft.

They had started to lower the rotational speed of the gravity section to allow the astronauts to begin adapting to Europan gravity from the normal 1 G Earth gravity.

It had been spinning at 1 G since they had left Earth; well, since the astronauts had left Earth.

To accelerate to the proper speeds, the *Odyssey* was sent alone across the Solar System to Venus and other planets for gravity assisted boosts and it was only during the last gravity assist by Earth that the astronauts docked with the mothership. It saved a long trip time for the astronauts and it was a solid test drive for the *Odyssey* before ISAF felt comfortable letting people get in. Let alone narwhals.

Lange chuckled at the idea. A small fluffy narwhal hung from the ceiling of the *Odyssey*'s hydroponics lab where she was working right now. It was a gift from one of her classmates at the Air Force's Space Officer accession course. J-D had briefed, with all the seriousness in the world, to his higher officers using an official PowerPoint that narwhals simply could not go into space. The water to store them could freeze, and their unicorn horn could pierce through the skin of the spacecraft and cause electrical problems. J-D then proceeded to brief about other animals that could not go into space, after clarifying that a cat launched by the French was probably 404 years old. The look of shock and derision from J-D's superiors was a stark contrast to Becky Lange's light chuckling right now. She didn't even try to continue with her experiment anymore, preferring instead to just laugh.

This feeling had been missing between the crew for some time now. So Lange decided to plan for a comedy movie night to try and pick up the crew's spirits. Leaving the plants in their peaceful, emotionless lives, Lange headed for the living room to procrastinate and peruse the movie library. She playfully jumped onto the couch and her jump looked like it took place in slow motion with the weaker force of gravity being exerted.

Hugo was waiting for Olivia looking at the electrical panel in question. He liked engineering and mechanics. It was simple. If you didn't arrange the wires properly, the lightbulb would not light. It wasn't nuanced like leadership. He thought back to another comment the Commander had told him: 'you're going to be alone.'

The future crew commander knew it was true. He had seen the Commander have to make decisions in secret without consultation. He thought back to the closed door discussions needed to get the *Odyssey* project back on track after someone had opened the floor to public voting on the details of the mission. He remembered how furious some of his crewmembers had been at the secrecy behind what was supposed to be a public, all-of-humanity mission. Just thinking of this reminded him how different everyone on his crew was. They were all very smart, but that's where their similarities stopped. Becky Lange had learned to accept the need for secrecy.

She had remembered the particular argument regarding flags. Some governments wanted their astronauts to wear their national flags on the space suits. Politicians were pandering to their constituents and had to look tough. But every detail was subject to the whims of hundreds of millions of people who knew nothing of space exploration or international relations. Some concessions had to be made, but no one could for fear of looking like a weak negotiator bowing to another foreign power. The doors had to remain closed for a group of people to make the right decisions for the good of the people instead of just the loudest interest group. There would be no national flag.

Her husband, Xavier, had helped by pointing out that the Lincoln Memorial on the National Mall of the American capital had almost never been built because a single politician had decided that the memorial would never be visited and the land should instead be sold to businesses. Fortunately, the politician had a change of heart by saying that "we tenderfeet perhaps ought not to have our way in matters of art." Lack of vision, fiscal conservatism and lack of political will had been the equation presented by university professors explaining why progress had trouble taking root in the US Congress, and what had stifled much of the science funding in the United States. Hugo certainly remembered the insane number of foreign scientists in the US on work visas.

"Staring has always solved all our problems," said Olivia, interrupting Hugo's train of thought that left him staring at an electrical panel.

He smiled at her, remembering that Olivia had refused to accept the need for secrecy. Plus, she was a foreigner in the eyes of American politicians. But a bright one that Hugo needed in order to fix the electrical panel he had been pensively staring at.

Hugo had certainly learned from the Commander to look beyond national interests when it came down to humanities. Caring for one another, exploring and expanding. These were human enterprises. Everyone deserved a chance to live. If their mission meant living could be on Europa, then he would lead his crew to the maximum of their capabilities and expertise.

The focus was on Europa and the analysis of how to establish a small research outpost on the Moon. The flight-plan followed by the Odyssey was following an orbit track that would allow the ship to act as a shuttle between Earth and the Jovian moon.

The idea of taking command of the first mission was enticing – Hugo couldn't deny it. There were no plans to land on any other system after Europa. He had hoped to maybe command one of the other missions beyond, but talk at ISAF revealed that even those missions might get axed in favor of the Europan colony. There would most likely not be any missions flying to Saturn, Neptune after this (nothing on Uranus). It was hard to conceive how far those worlds were from each other. It took a little over 2 years for a probe to get from Earth to Jupiter. It took another year and a half to get from Jupiter to Saturn, and that's if their orbits were aligned properly. Jupiter was pretty much hallway between the Earth and Saturn.

This mission to Europa had to count. For the foreseeable future, it was the only presence Humanity would have in deep space.

Chapter 7

The Commander sat at the communal, rectangular table with the rest of her crew.

"How was everyone's day today?"

Everyone nodded and mumbled a 'fine', just like everyone always answered.

"I'm putting on pause tomorrow's scientific experiments tasked."

That got everyone looking at the Commander. So she continued to explain. "One of the reasons we have those experiments is to keep us busy during the transit voyage, and we have to do a few other things to keep us busy."

"I'm actually really good at keeping myself busy," commented Puff. "X-Box, X-Men comics, X-rated movies. You really don't need to add anything if you cancel something."

"We need to be filming each other," continued the Commander.

"Was it the X-movies that convinced you? I'm totally game, but I have to warn you, it's going to make Olivia and Becky really jealous..."

"Cut it out, Puff," answered the Commander. "We're going to act out events as if we were on Europa. Some of us are going to take panels off the *Columbiad* tomorrow morning to re-create the interior here in the gravity sections; we'll probably use the GYM, and with that set up, we'll film out dozens, actually, hundreds of update messages for ISAF to rebroadcast to the rest of the world."

The whole crew frowned in confusion.

"Why not just send over the messages when we're *actually* on Europa?" asked Hugo.

"Two reasons: First, I will not be there. We need footage of me on Europa. Second: to ensure no one suspects we are headed back to Earth early. The messages we record here and on Europa will be slowly sent over the length of our return trip home. You need to have me in there so that it looks like normal ops. This will allow Dr. Montsegur and the rest of the planet to believe that we are still doing everything as planned. We'll send some of the messages we record here while you're still on Europa, to get people used to whatever set up we come up with here. But even after you launch to come home with the Russians and Indians, you'll keep this trickle of pre-recorded messages going to keep Earth believing you are still exploring. So this is what I want us to work on for the next couple of days. Ahmed and Olivia, first thing tomorrow I want you guys to slow down the gravity section to generate the same force of gravity as is present on Europa. This will allow us to walk realistically: as if we were on the low-gravity moon. Besides, I'm sure you wouldn't mind getting used to the practice."

"Not to mention moving the pieces of the *Columbiad* around will be easier if everything is lighter," agreed Becky.

"Speaking of practice," added Hugo. "If it's ok with you, Commander, I'd like to steal a few of the crew at a time whenever they're not recording fake Europa breaking news to spend some time in the simulator with them."

"That's a good idea," agreed the Commander. "With me gone, you guys may need to help cover for me and this includes in some of the flight duties. So more time in the sim with Hugo."

Puff moaned.

"You could instead help Becky with recycling our waste into the plant feed?" suggested the Commander.

"No, I'm going to be too busy in the sim with Hugo," instantly said Puff, retracting his moan. "Isn't that right Hugo?"

The crew continued with their table talk like they usually did, talking about meaningless things such as a comedy film or past experiences with different jobs. Aki, Olivia, Ahmed and the Commander were still surprised with the amount of gossip Americans were willing to thrash out. According to their American counterparts, there was a name that when given unto a child simply cursed them. The name Virginia was just not a good one to bestow in the United States. The state itself was not too problematic (although the Western one was the source of considerable derision from most Americans and was statistically a land of highly uneducated and obese hillbillies) but the people named Virginia, even though highly educated and working for the some of the planet's most advanced militaries and space programs still got Becky and Puff riled up. Puff even called it a condition: having the Virginias, which vacillated between being a victim of being too much with a Virginia (despair, frustration, impatience, behavioral change to violence, eye pain due to eye rolling, fake sleeping, frequent repetition of statements told) to being a Virginia (total lack of social cues, inability to control vocal volume, frequent vacation requests, extreme narcissism, absolute innocence in all problems in life, acute emotional fluctuations).

The Commander tolerated the gossip mainly because it was Puff making Becky laugh after a long day and Becky deserved to be happy even if it made the Commander uncomfortable hearing this gossip.

But with the end of dinner approaching, the crew started to break away for their own personal time.

The next morning, the crew started to break down a few panels of the *Columbiad* and floated them to the portion of the zero-gravity corridor that accessed the ladder leading to the gym facilities. Puff and Aki stayed in the gym, looking up the ladder while the Commander and Hugo slowly pushed the panels down the tunnel, the artificial gravity slowly taking hold and pulling the panels toward Puff and Aki for them to catch. Ahmed had reprogrammed the gravity-ring they spent their time in to reproduce the same gravity that Europa generated. The panels were easy to catch, as were the bags of water Becky had gathered to simulate water recycling and the food they would sometimes eat in front of the camera to simulate working late.

By the end of the morning, the cameras were set up to present multiple angles of the set up. The different cameras, thanks to the different angles, were filming what looked like completely different compartments from each other, even though they were all in the same room. The crew was getting a crash course on cinematography and set-design, but they were satisfied with the setup and started to bring in some of their experiments. The person that would spend the most time in there was going to be the Commander, but one of the corridors that bypassed the gym-now-turned-*Columbiad*-set was condemned. The Commander asked the blast door in that corridor to be sealed, forcing everyone on the crew to walk through the set while the Commander was in there filming whatever it was she was doing. Forcing everyone through the set would allow everyone else on Earth to see the rest of the crew casually passing by and attribute their presence with the Commander. That was critical, particularly after they separated, and she headed back to Earth on her own. After the *Columbiad* separated from the *Odyssey*, there would be no more opportunities for the

Commander to be caught on camera with the rest of the crew. To fool Dr. Montsegur, they were going to have to convincingly be all together.

The same afternoon, Becky walked onto the temporary set with a few containers that were designed to hold ice samples from Europa.

"Hey Sophia," started Becky under the watchful eyes of the cameras. "Here are the containers for the upcoming EVA."

"Ok, thanks. Can you submit your report of the Illium chasm quickly? Or at least give a recap to Aki and Hugo? They're going to head out in about an hour or two to do another survey."

"Sure. I'll head over and do that right now."

"Thanks!"

Becky left from the field of view of the cameras, and she wasn't going to go talk to Aki or Hugo. But for future viewers, it was convincing enough.

A few minutes later, the Commander changed shirts, dimmed one of the lights and sat next to Hugo talking about depleted fuel levels.

Another hour later, the Commander was cleaning out her Europan suit which had been dirtied with oil. She had just returned from a convincing repair of the *Columbiad*.

"Sophia didn't get enough video of me today!" pleaded Becky.

"I did," replied the Commander with a grin. "Go practice."

Becky groaned. The last attempt to get out of having to conduct a sim ride with Hugo failed. Hugo wasn't bad, but it was just annoying to be in the simulators to watch over the computers that were going to do everything for them anyways except for the potential last minute of flight.

As Becky moved to toward the *Columbiad*, climbing the ladder out of the gravity sections to the central tunnel where she floated to the hatch, the biologist thought back to the discussions about driverless cars that had dominated the radio waves a decade ago.

Fortunately, the questions of whether or not to save the occupants of the vehicle or the pedestrians was resolved. Even more fortunately, there was no one on Europa to hit with a self-driving car.

The *Columbiad* was, of course, fully automated. But just like with most other major systems, everyone on the crew had to have familiarity with the switches and different commands that could be sent to the flight computers. Becky didn't really enjoy that part of the astronaut training – it was tedious, and you had to think like the computers were programmed. She would have been happy to get out of the lessons teaching her about computer logic and how to think like the computers. She had been told it was similar to biology – induce different scenarios and plants grow differently. She didn't agree with those who told her that.

"Becky?" called out the Commander from the top hatch down into the *Columbiad*. Her head was just hovering, floating there. "I need you to check the water-flow valve in hydroponics."

"Thank goodness!" said Becky as she instantly undid her harness from the cockpit and bolted up the tunnel. When she passed the Commander, she did a flip against the back wall and went down another tunnel-ladder back to the gravity section. The Commander decided to float down to Hugo as he powered down the *Columbiad* systems. The simulation was now over.

"How's are the landing sims going?" as the Commander took a seat in what was supposed to be hers to take when they were to land on Europa.

"Pretty good. I mean the ship flies itself, I'm just running through manual processes, but most of the crew still knows what they're doing," sighed Hugo from his own seat in the *Columbiad*. "This is going to be a boring ride down."

"Well there's a reason why there are no pilots on the crew. Like you said: it flies itself. I doubt the descent will be boring. You'll have Jupiter or Europa in your field of view."

"I know," smirked Hugo. "I'm sorry. I didn't mean to casually toss this opportunity that you won't be able to experience with us."

"Oh don't worry. I don't really care to walk on Europa. I care more about the potential discoveries."

"Well you'll have your name on whatever it is we discover here. I mean, you pretty much got us here."

"ISAF and the ground guys got us here. I babysat you, that is all. Your accomplishments are yours, not your babysitter is. But thank you, though. I know putting a name at the bottom of a paper is a pretty competitive, big deal. So thank you."

"Yeah. I guess the Russian commander will want to share his name on there, too then, huh?"

"Sergei Komarov? No, I don't think he'll want any of that. I see him more as a going into reclusion after returning to Earth. I think that's all he wants: to be left alone."

"Hmm. Well hopefully he's a bit of a recluse on the *Otkrytiye*, too."

The Commander chuckled.

"Oh that reminds me," she said. "Komarov may feel a little resentful about what I'm going to do."

"What? Why would he ever not be happy with that?"

"Because it was his idea and he originally called me to take his crew. In fact, they were ready to all kill themselves, but I presented them with the option we're doing now. Since the *Otkrytiye* was already closer to Europa, the course adjustment would have been too complicated and risky, diminishing the chances of mission success. Just be aware of that when you interact with him, and please don't let the others get all prideful on me. Sergei, even though he may seem like another one of those crazy Russians, is a very intelligent man who shares many of our qualities."

"Such as?" muttered Hugo with a doubtful tone.

"Do the job you're told, be creative, study hard... Just like the most serious kid in the class. And if you're fortunate enough to get on his good side, he'll probably tell you some jokes and old war stories."

"He was in a war?"

Hugo was a pacifist and Becky and him had originally had some issues when they first started training.

"That's not the point," deflected the Commander from answering the question. "The point was simply be aware of his original interest in being the hero. So be sensitive to that. He'll be your Commander soon enough. When you board the *Otkrytiye*."

"That's a good point," admitted Hugo.

Hugo was in fact rather surprised to feel relief at the thought that this Sergei fellow was going to be the Commander again. With the Russian in command, Hugo would be freed from making the unpopular decisions...

"Don't forget that you'll still be in charge of our crew," reminded the Commander to Hugo. "You'll answer to Sergei Komarov, but the others from the *Odyssey* will be looking to you for guidance on what to do, how to act and for you to stand up for them."

Hugo's shoulders slumped a little. The ridiculous 'burden' of command.

"I know," acknowledged Hugo.

"Alright. I'm gonna let you get back to what you were doing. I just really came in to rescue Becky from you. She hates the idea of entering Europa."

"You know your crew well."

"You know them just as well. You'll see."

Hugo nodded his head, hoping that it was true. The Commander floated away, leaving Hugo with his thoughts and the ship he would soon be commanding.

Lange had returned to her room and sat down. The idea of having to prepare messages for the future had gotten her thinking that there was still an inherent risk to their future endeavors. Xavier had suggested before the launch that Becky record dozens of messages for their kids in case something were to happen to her. They would still have messages from their mother in the distant future.

But throughout the preparations for the mission, she refused. Lange had steadfastly refused to accept that something could happen to her, and Xavier didn't want to worry her by insisting. If he had kept asking, it would have implied that he expected her to die. Which he didn't.

The reality was that one of their original crewmembers was about to embark on what could reasonably be construed as a suicide mission. Sighing, the young astronaut stared at her computer and started to think about what she was going to say.

She sobbed.

Becky Lange was preparing to send messages to her children. They were intended in case she was never to see them again. If she wasn't going to be there to help her daughter prepare for her wedding day or her college graduation, or to help her son pick out an engagement ring or finish his homework.

Silently crying, Becky cursed herself for being so selfish.

She had left them all behind for the sake of her exploratory desires. She had kept repeating she wanted to be an astronaut. Sniffling, she took a deep breath. It didn't matter now. The biologist was aboard the *Odyssey* at this point, and she could still correct her mistakes.

Taking a deep breath, she started a recording for Xavier. She explained her change of heart and how he was right. "Don't let that get to your head," she smiled before continuing. Different videos were intended for different portions of their lives. They would be there to supplement the Dear John letter she had prepared for everyone in case she was killed. That message was already in the hands of ISAF and its estate attorneys. She remembered having to struggle with how to say good-bye to him, but for him. The reality was that she was going to be dead. Xavier would be the one that would have to deal with that fact. And the children. Should she tell him to re-marry? How should she convey forgiveness for the fights they had in the past?

So for the next few hours, Becky Lange imagined the future life of her children. Their greatest triumphs and the most perilous failures. She tried to keep a laughing face and a tender voice, but sorrow still sometimes trickled through. Lange rerecorded a few of the messages. But at least they were there.

Chapter 8

"Let's go over the numbers," said the Commander as they all looked up to Hugo, standing in front of a large flat-screen with the details of their descent to Europa.

"Ok, so we'll have 45 seconds of spare gas before we need to put down the *Columbiad* or abort and return to orbit."

"Wow, 45 seconds? That's a full minute and 15 seconds less than original. That's so much shorter," called out an astonished Ahmed.

"Well we don't have much backup, unfortunately,"

"Break it down, math boy," said Puff.

Hugo sighed. "We have to land within 4 hours of walking time from the Indo-Russian spacecraft given the EVA suit's limitations..."

"We have 5 hours of suit time. Plus another hour for backup," called out Puff.

"The book says we can only factor in 20% in case the terrain we're crossing ends up being more difficult to navigate."

"Ok," interrupted the Commander. "Suit O_2 is not the concern right now," she added, trying to keep them on topic.

"Right, sorry. So we have to land where we plan to land, but if something goes wrong during the descent, we need extra fuel to catch back up with the *Odyssey*. Originally, the *Odyssey* was on a different trajectory and velocity, but things are obviously different now. Which means we would need extra fuel. The only source is from our descent fuel. So to be able to catch up to the *Odyssey*, we need to limit our descent time."

"What's the backup plan if we can't get back to the *Odyssey*?" asked Aki.

"Well depending on the problem we face, another option is that we land and walk to the Indo-Russian ship."

"And if the problem says we can't land?"

"We head to orbit and wait for 3 months until the *Otkrytiye* rendezvous' with us. But then the fuel is really short because we would be slightly off-plane and we'd have to execute an extra burn to get in the proper position."

"Wouldn't that be a problem anyways then? Even after we land?" asked Becky.

"No. If we land, we can adjust our launch to head in the right direction from the launch point, so we'll be ok if we land as planned."

"But we if we don't land as planned," added Puff, "two of our backups are dependent on the Indian and the Russians opening the door for us."

"They will," reassured Becky. "They have no quarrel with us and we're not countries at war or anything like that. If they abandon us, you can bet the diplomatic results would be catastrophic for them."

"Not to mention illegal, per the UN Astronaut in Distress treaty..."

"And we don't have a choice," interrupted the Commander. "The Russians are the only ride you have to guarantee time on Europa. We better all start trusting each other. Or Dr. Montsegur might have a point."

"Ok so what are the plans, in recap then?" asked Ahmed.

"Before we get to gate 1, here," said Hugo showing on the screen a dot located 800 km above the surface of Europa, "if something goes wrong, we execute a burn and catch up to the *Odyssey*. After gate 1, if we cannot land, we burn back into orbit and wait for the *Otkrytiye*. Finally, after touchdown, if we have an emergency as we land, we'll clear the *Columbiad* and walk to the Indo-Russian ship which should be landing right next door."

"Can the Indo-Russian ship take-off with us and our extra mass in it?" asked Aki.

"Yes. If we get inside and dump our suits and give up most samples, we can launch. The challenge will be seatbelts. We'll probably be confined to their bunks while the Indians and Russians sit in their crash-resistant seats, but since we're launching from a low gravity world, we should be perfectly fine."

Hugo was comfortable with the idea of lying in a bed during the launch given the weak gravity of Europa. The thin atmosphere also meant that there would be very little if any turbulence other than the rattling of the engines, which meant he was confident it would be a smooth ride. Puff, knowing more about engines, doubted how smooth it would be since the Russians weren't known for caring about comfort or mitigating turbulence when designing spacecraft, but he also agreed that it would be a smooth ride even if they weren't in a harnessed seat. In fact, they might have gotten the better end of the deal: just lie down and enjoy the ride. Hugo and Puff looking completely fine with the idea helped Becky and the others completely believe that there were no issues either.

"This means you'll be in your EVA suits during the descent," added the Commander. "Originally, being suited up for the descent to Europa wasn't even considered because you would have had nowhere to go. But now you do."

Becky Lange didn't really care other than it might get a little warm during the descent. But it wasn't like they would have to fly the *Columbiad*: it literally flew itself."

"Barton labs has already run all the calculations about these plans," continued Hugo. "We're good. Not by much, but it's all possible, even if it's beyond mission parameters."

"Which means it's beyond the minimums already recommended by ISAF when they built the spacecraft," emphasized the Commander. "So if the gauge reads empty, don't even think of saying 'engineers always leave a little extra fuel at the bottom.' They already took into account that little bit of extra. You have zero slop left."

"You're sloppy," grinned Puff to Ahmed.

"Get out," sighed the Commander.

Puff groaned but listened and left the dining room.

"We're done. All of you get out," added the Commander. "Unless you have questions. Then Hugo can answer them."

The crew broke apart and started to head for their last few duties of the day, mainly cleaning and sealing their personal quarters and packing. They originally were going to be coming back to the *Odyssey*, but with that plan out the airlock, the crew wanted to make the ship spotless for the lone crewmember that was going to be left behind and keep the few things that they really cared about aboard the ship. They would most likely never return to the *Odyssey* after leaving tomorrow. Unless something went terribly wrong.

After dinner, half the crew found themselves in the dining room around a pot of tea. The other half of the crew was finalizing the ship for the long trip back to Earth for the Commander. The lights were dimmed to emphasize the evening 'hour' even in deep space. With the mood came quiet smiles and light discussions. They mainly all stared at their mugs wafting a warm steam into the recycled air.

"You know, if I were the one going on the *Odyssey* to get that Montsegur..." piped up Puff.

"Doctor Montsegur," corrected the Commander.

"Yes, him," continued Puff, "I would make everyone on Earth give me some money beforehand. I mean seriously, I don't think it's right for people who didn't work or contribute to this space program at all to be rescued."

"They didn't do anything to deserve this!" protested Ahmed with agreement from Aki.

"So what? That's life. You don't think those well off already have shelters built? They worked to ensure their survival. No, the only reason why the boss is doing this is to save the poor guys who don't have anything. The people who usually don't work and live off of their governments, and us by extension."

"I don't think you're in a position to tell me why I'm doing this," sighed the Commander. "Thank you for sharing your point of view Puff, but I'm ending it here."

"What? I'm not allowed to have my own opinion?"

"You may have an opinion, you may not voice it. Not when you try to convince others that the alternative to paying you is an asteroid being lobbed to Earth and killing people who are obviously powerless."

"Free speech, anyone?"

"Free speech is your American way to defend that you can say anything you want, but as you know, yelling fire in a crowded theater remains illegal because it is against the common good, just like lies were illegalized during World War I in the United States to protect your war effort. While I certainly believe that most aboard do not share your idea of earning life, I will remind you that your free-speech right is a responsibility, it is a right to protect you so you may call out your government if it becomes too oppressive, and as I just explained, it can again be restricted if it is against the common good or simply not true."

"By who?"

"Me," said the Commander.

Puff was about to say something, but the Commander interrupted him again.

"You want to now make a statement about your rights, but you know this is not the place and not something that is worth discussing," she calmly said looking into his eyes. "And you know it's true. Because when it comes down to ideas that are designed to prevent access and rights for some on our world, you are all for it until it affects you. But we both know you would cry foul if it ever touched you. This, right now, is an example. You want people on Earth to pay to live instead of only you being the person paying and others living off of you, yet I am here to restrict something in your life, your voice, and you whine. As I said, it is not something you need to discuss any longer."

"Whatever," grumbled Puff. "All I'm saying is you should consider creating a bank account with a trust fund for your family or something."

"I'm gonna go check the internal valve pressure on the helium disks," announced Ahmed. "Puff, you want to come with me?"

Puff understood the message and quietly left the dining room.

"Please be nice to me before you leave," smiled Aki. "I don't want to remember you as this cold, logical mathematics machine. I don't like maths."

The Commander chuckled with the others around the table.

"Aki, I want you to record these events."

"Oh?" she gasped in surprise.

"People need to know that we are not perfect. Let the historians decide if I made the right choice tonight."

"You are a wise leader," smiled Aki with a slight bow. "You are a like an Emperor Meiji, but woman."

"Who's that?" asked Olivia as she walked into the dining room to get her evening ration.

"He was a Japanese emperor that successfully defended against a Russian invasion. Japan was still pre-industrial and Russia thought it would be an easy victory – but the Japanese were very well informed of Russian tactics and abilities, subsequently crushing them."

"Huh...," continued Olivia, not impressed. "Why are you clowns talking about that?" she grinned.

"We've been together for a year already, not counting training," replied the Commander. "How are the medical supplies?"

"Tip top. Becky is just packing the final plant leaves in the *Columbiad* for tomorrow afternoon."

"Speaking of which," added Becky Lange as she walked in to rejoin the rest of the crew. "I just checked the schedule for tomorrow morning. It just says brunch until we're supposed to board the *Columbiad*."

"Indeed," replied the Commander with a grin.

"But I checked it an hour ago and it still had us with sims, filter replacements and..."

"Becky," smiled the Commander. "I'm going to have a lot of time on my hands to do those things. Don't rob me of this opportunity to stay busy. You already just robbed me of the surprise of giving the morning off for everyone tomorrow."

Becky groaned at her mistake. She hated surprises and had a tendency to ruin surprises planned by others. She had even guessed portions of what Xavier had planned for his proposal to her. And it had started with one of their first dates. He had to learn to live with it.

The Commander had no such need – she wasn't beholden to Becky's every whim.

Chapter 9

"Springs unlocked," called out Olivia.

"We're loose," confirmed the Commander. "Radar's up... 2 meters per second sep velocity. Those springs definitely gave us a boost. I probably didn't need to fire the RCS," he muttered to himself.

"Checklist discipline," sighed Ahmed, trying to reassure Hugo. "They'll get you for that. You can lie, steal, cheat and screw the intern. But not following the checklist, they'll get you for that. So if we're a little fast, it's not your fault. We simply followed the checklist."

"You're cleared the omni," said Sophia over the radio, observing from the *Odyssey*.

"Although you should probably just thrust to slow down a bit there, Evil Knievel," added Ahmed.

"Computer confirms this," replied the Commander. "Computer is on pitch program. Pitching up, 2.5 degrees per second."

The *Columbiad* started a backflip as it continued to move away from *Odyssey*. To someone just immobile in space, the two spacecraft were performing this dance while traveling at bullet speeds. But to Sophia, observing the *Columbiad* from one of the portholes aboard the *Odyssey*, the two spaceships were slowly separating, like a slow motion view of lover's hands slipping away from each other. Sophia knew the entire procedure was all on the *Columbiad* and its computers now.

Through the windows of both spacecraft, Sophia saw Hugo, the new Commander, looking up at his computer screens. But the flipping ship quickly put them out of view. Hugo was the last human she would see in person for the next year. Maybe for the rest of her life.

"Commander Hugo Evrard and crew of the *Columbiad*, this is *Odyssey*. I see a good pitch over. Your shield is intact. Fair winds and clear skies," broadcast Sophia to the *Columbiad*.

Without waiting for a response, Sophia shut off the speakers and communications systems aboard the *Odyssey*. She hated emotional goodbyes and didn't want to hear anymore mushy stuff coming from her former crewmates. If for some reason the *Columbiad* had to return to the *Odyssey*, the Commander could still press the CALL button on his communications panel which would notify Sophia aboard.

But the original flight plan never called for anyone to remain aboard the *Odyssey*. Everyone was supposed to travel to Europa while the *Odyssey* would go into a variety of planetary laps around the Jovian system. Because no one was scheduled to remain aboard the mother-ship, Sophia didn't have much to do but simply watch the *Columbiad* automatically fly itself to the surface of Europa. The astronaut would probably not have much to do in case the spaceship tried to re-dock with the *Odyssey*, either.

Using its internal sensors and inertial navigation units, the *Columbiad* oriented itself away from its mother ship that had gotten them so close to their target moon.

Europa poured a blue glow in any room that had windows looking to the outside moon. The blue-ish, icy world took up the view of the windows and seemed magnificent. The icy peaks of the mountains ridges looked majestic, and the thin atmospheric layer glowed orange over the horizon.

As she observed the view, Sophia suddenly felt loneliness drape itself over her. Hugo was now the master of the *Columbiad*. The title of commander was transferred to him. Sophia had lost her crew. It was gone, not just symbolically in terms of responsibility, but also physically. The explorers were headed down to the surface of the bright moon hanging outside her window in the darkness of black, inky space. Sophia was completely alone. Everywhere she went aboard this ship from now on, there would be no one. Absolute freedom and privacy. And nobody to ever interact with her live.

Becky was back in her small room aboard the *Columbiad*, which was even more cramped than the one aboard the *Odyssey*. It was designed to be smaller than the *Odyssey* for two reasons. The first one was obvious: minimize space to minimize the size of the ship required to land on Europa. The second, though, was psychological. The crew was supposed to live in the *Columbiad* for about a year, but still had to look forward to a long trip home aboard the *Odyssey*. ISAF designers had discovered through research that moving into a larger room from a smaller one uplifted morale and spirits incredibly high. That would help the crew stay positive during the long trip home after they returned to the *Odyssey*, giving them a larger space to retreat to if they needed to.

Fortunately, Becky was going to be living in the *Columbiad* for a year and wouldn't be spending an additional year traveling home, since their stay on Europa was going to be shortened. But they first had to land on Europa. They would hopefully be there in six hours, but in the meantime, she wrote a quick email to her husband.

While working on it, she caught her breath when she saw Jupiter outside the porthole. It was there, as familiar as ever. She couldn't see the Great Red spot – it was probably on the other side of the planet. The shadow where day ended and night started was a perfectly straight line. It cut through all the colors of the planet: the red and orange stripes that sandwiched white clouds that travelled in the opposite direction. The parallel bands that lapped the gas giant were different from the chaotic clouds of Earth.

Even so close to that world, Becky had trouble understanding how big the planet was. She had been told numerous times how big it was. The numbers, the comparisons etc. The few hours between separation and the landing meant everyone had some time to themselves to relax. Most took the time to observe the massive planet they were not going to be landing on (and perhaps no one ever would).

Jupiter was *enormous*. Everywhere... regarding everything.

Driving a car around the top of the clouds would take 142 days driving at 80 miles per hour for 24 hours. Earth would be encircled in 13 days.

The crew had heard it all – but when she saw it outside, she simply didn't realize how big it was because she couldn't fathom how far they still were from it. The perspective was difficult to size up.

What she did remember clearly was that if it weren't for the shielding on the ship (which was considerable and contained layers of gels, ceramics and other classified things she didn't originally care to learn about), the magnetic field emanating from the planet (22,000 times stronger than on Earth – another set of numbers so large no one could really understand) would fry and damage a lot of things including her body. But the shielding allowed her to stare at the striations that were the colorful winds, traveling at hundreds of miles an hour.

Staring out her small window from the ship, Becky was getting lost focusing on the details of those clouds. Some looked like they tried to poke into another band, with others churned at the edges without ever leaving their set band – like a racetrack around the planet...

"15 minutes to boarding," said an announcement over the PA.

Snapping back to reality, Becky quickly hit the send button to email her handwritten message and walked to the ladder that would take her to the changing room. The faster she got there, the faster she could get her mind off of her family and the approaching entry interface. Instead, she could focus on her suit and the checklist to prepare it. Which is exactly what she did when she got to the bay that housed their gear.

An hour later she was suited up and floated into her seat aboard the *Columbiad*. Ahmed was already inside the cockpit prepping the ship. Random whirring and pumps would come on, some fluids (Becky didn't care to know which ones) could be heard flowing as she fastened her seatbelt. Aki was doing the same thing, but they didn't say much to each other.

"Let's light this firecracker," said Puff as he flipped into his seat. "Where's Hugo? A ship CANNOT GO DOWN WITHOUT HER CAPTAIN!" he shouted down the tunnel to a Hugo who was also arriving.

"I'm here, Puff."

Olivia didn't appreciate the 'going down' comment. She knew it was a fact that they were going down to the surface of the moon, but she knew the numbers and wasn't comfortable with them. They were arriving at Mach 27 and would be breaking in seven minutes to just 9 miles per hour. The thought of what could possibly go wrong had troubled her enough that Aki had prescribed her a mild sedative to help her stay calm. Becky was offered the same thing, but Becky Lange was more concerned about being alert when they were going to land on Europa.

INITIATE LANDING PROCEDURE: Y/N

"Puff?" called out the Commander after the prompt appeared on their screens.

"Ship is green across the board," acknowledged the engineer.

"I concur," agreed Aki.

"Ship is green and stable, initiating landing procedure," announced the Commander for the black-boxes and the microphones that were automatically left on during the critical phases of flight. Those microphones were relaying all the data back to Earth, which could help an investigation in case something went wrong.

The Commander entered Y and enter, and nothing happened except for the prompt disappeared.

The ship was still on course and trajectory and there was no need to change that. All that happened was the computer now had permission to begin its descent at the appropriate moment further down the line instead of doing another lap in orbit. But there was no action-packed rocket booster ignition or soul-crushing turbulence. Something Lange felt thankful for.

For now.

Two hours, 2 orbits and one touchdown later, Becky's personal screen next to her seat flashed a message from Earth. It was odd, since there was a 30 minute delay in messages, which meant the message had been sent 30 minutes before now. Thirty minutes before their historic landing on a celestial body that wasn't the Earth. Becky opened the message.

Congratulations! We're very proud of you, Europan! X.

The Commander also spoke up from his seat.

"Olivia. Please communicate with ISAF that we made a safe landing and let the Russians know where we landed."

Lange realized that Xavier had sent his message without knowing if she had landed safely. She wondered how he would feel if they had not landed safely. He probably would have just typed another message saying 'jk lol. Number-sign Better luck next time.'

"Where did we land?" asked Olivia.

"I'll get that to you in a second," answered Ahmed. "Here are the coordinates," he said as he send a message on their computers. "We'll send a message to the Indians and Russians when the satellite makes another pass."

"In the meantime, VORTAC and TriDAR are on and broadcasting our position to them so that they can hopefully land nearby."

"Well, this is all amazing, but now that we're here, I'm ready to go for my first walk outside a spaceship in over a year," said Puff as he unbuckled himself from his seat and jumped out of it. "Come on, Aki. I know you love a good romantic walk... on the ice."

The Commander thought about it and agreed. The Russo Indian ship was on track to land as scheduled. He shut off the clocks on the *Columbiad* before rising from her seat.

"We're already in our suits, let's go ahead and step outside. I think we could all use a walk."

After the Commander stepped down the ladder and onto the landing strut foot-pad, he threw open a long, red piece of carpet onto the surface of Europa.

"The red carpet has been laid out," he said over his radio. "Come on down."

The rest of the crew came down the ladder, taking a moment to examine the magnificent desolation from their spacecraft. Different shades of white and blue topped with a dark, inky blackness above it all. It looked like they had landed not far from a small frozen bay flanked by steep black and white cliffs that dove into the ice. Snow covered almost everything except for the steepest rocky ledges. A mini volcano-caldera-looking island was visible not far from the flat ice-sheet that looked like the frozen lake. It all looked peaceful.

Pure.

When the team was on the red carpet, they all together stepped from the red carpet onto the surface of Europa.

Chapter 10

The Commander stepped into Puff's alcove-sized room finding him playing on a video game console.

"How are we looking for our fuel reserves?" asked the Commander.

"We can make a site-to-site jump if it turns out we need to," replied Puff as he grabbed a tablet and handed it to the Commander without taking his eyes off his video game. It showed the calculations of launching the *Columbiad* a few hundred feet to glide to a point closer to the Indo-Russian landing site with a satisfying green box that read ACCEPTABLE, before Puff continued: "But given the readings we're getting from their beacon, I reckon we're close enough that we don't need to. I would prefer to keep what we have left-over for the launch to their spaceship."

"How will these extra reserves affect our launch? Is it going to make us too heavy with the profile their spacecraft has to come pick us up?"

"Not a chance. Our weight is more than good even if we're performing a rendezvous at a higher altitude than anticipated."

"Ok. I'm going to suit up with Becky and Aki to head over to attempt a meeting with the Russians and Indians. I want you to work with Olivia and the rest of the team to get this ship ready to fly."

"What? I'm busy."

"With what?"

"Protecting the *Columbiad* from these demons I'm slaying," finished Puff as he pressed a button on his vintage Nintendo Switch.

The Commander rolled his eyes.

"Besides, don't you guys think it would be smart to have me come along to ensure the best diplomatic relations?" asked Puff.

"That's exactly why you're not coming, unofficially."

"Hurtful," replied Puff without a hint of offense. "And the official one?"

"We need someone who can steer the *Columbiad* to us if we run into problems and can't walk back to the lander."

Puff sighed. "That sounds like more work. I might just leave you out there."

"We leave when the engines are declared ready by you," said the Commander as he took a ladder back up to the flight deck. "Get cracking at it."

Puff let out a loud "ugh" for the rest of the crew to hear but got started on his work.

The team of three explorers from the *Columbiad* walked along a waving frozen sea of ice, the massive Jovian gas giant lighting their path.

"Remind me again," groaned Becky as she walked along, "why with all our advances in spaceships and computers and self-important apps like Facebook, you'd think we could have made spacesuits that are less bulky than the monstrosities worn by the Apollo astronauts on the lunar surface? In fact, why don't we have the ones the guys on the Moon are wearing today?"

"You really want me to remind you?" said the Commander.

"Well no. but given that you're not really chatting about anything else and you've banned us from stopping to perform any experiments, I think it's incumbent on you, dear sir, to ensure our radio communications remain open."

"Very well," replied the Commander. "First off, I am not allowing research work to take place right now because we need to make sure we can make it to the Russo-Indian lander on our supply of air. Stopping to look at ice or the stars would deplete that air that we're trying to maximize. And second of all, you're wearing this thick suit compared to those guys on the Moon because of that big guy up there," continued the Commander, pointing up to Jupiter, hanging in the dark sky. They could all see the clouds swirling around the circle that was the largest planet in the Sol solar system. "That giant failed-of-a-star planet generates a pretty powerful magnetic field that has trapped dangerous levels of radiation into belts surrounding it. Given Europa's prime position traversing those regions, we must have extra radiation protection."

"Oh... that's right," said Becky.

The conversation again stopped into silence and the trio continued to walk forward, following a path laid before them by a computer heads-up-display inside their helmet visors, guiding them along an otherwise barren landscape. Each of them also had tiny rear-view mirrors above their right eyebrow to see their colleagues walking fifteen feet behind them. They had to walk with so much distance apart from each other in case the surface wasn't stable. Becky knew that no one had ever explored the ice world, but her experiences on Earth had revealed that anytime you were dealing with ice-sheets, you could also be dealing with crevasses. Or chasms. Which were synonymous to death, so she abided by the spacing requirements. If one of them were to fall into a crevasse, the other two would act as anchor points. The suits would detect a sudden fall with their internal accelerometers even faster than the person falling, immediately sending out a signal for the other suits connected to anchor down. That's why jumping wasn't allowed. They would have to shut down the "fall protocol" to make sure they didn't activate it accidently while hopping and skipping along the moon's surface. And it just wouldn't be professional to do so. Maybe in the 1970s it was cool to just bounce around, but in the 21st century days of exploration, professionalism was the order of the day. Or so Becky was told.

After a few hours of walking, the trio finally saw the *Vimāna*.

"Wow," said Becky. "They really did copy a lot of ISAF's designs," pointing out the extreme resemblance the Russian and Indian ship had with the *Columbiad*.

The curvature of the small moon meant the lander was closer than it appeared, but the trio still wished it was even closer. Hugo couldn't help but realize that it was a towering structure – a shelter, built by man. The first time since this world had been created, eons ago, that a structure like this would ever be seen on Europa... It was comforting to see. A familiar sight in an otherwise unfamiliar, barren moon. A familiar sight, because of intellectual property theft, too. Another concept that Europa probably never had to deal with.

"*Vimāna*, this is Hugo Evrard, from the *Columbiad*. I am here with Doctors Becky Lange and Aki Suru, and we have your lander in sight. Is it safe to approach? We are on the 032 radial at 1.6 nautical miles."

A few moments later, the trio heard the response from the Indo-Russian team.

"Hello, friends," said a visible smiling voice. "Yes, it's ok for you to come over. Kindly be careful when you approach, we have installed some experiments."

"Understood, thank you."

About 30 minutes later, the three members from the *Columbiad* were at the foot of the Indo-Russian lander.

"*Vimāna*, we're at your..."

The airlock light turned from red to green, signaling they could enter.

After stepping into the airlock, the trio noticed how similar the interior was to the *Columbiad*. But they still felt in a strange ship – the writing was in Cyrillic and Hindi.

"You may remove your helmets," said a voice over the radio, confirming the readings that the three had learned from their own ship.

Obeying, Becky, Hugo and Aki all took off their helmets. Soon after, the door leading to the *Vimāna* was unlocked with a slight horn sounding. The large latch was lifted and the door was swung open.

Standing in front of them was a tall, bearded man. He had a chiseled chin that could still be distinguished through his dark, black hairs. His eyes were almost soulless. Dark brown and piercing, it was clear that no one from the *Columbiad* would want to doubt his authority. Hugo had no doubt that standing in front of them, dressed in a blue flight suit with a Russian flagged patch was the commander of the Indo-Russian crew.

"Hi," started Hugo. "I'm Hugo Evrard."

"I am Captain second rank Konstantin Komarov," replied the man with a deep voice.

"Where is everyone?" asked Becky, noticing no one behind Komarov.

"They are out conducting exploration and collection. Less time on the moon means more work. Now, you have proven walking between ships is possible."

"Correct," replied Hugo. "Here are the numbers from our chief engineer," he added, handing over a small memory drive. "They show the parameters for the *Columbiad* to launch to the *Otkrytiye* when we add your crew's mass, in the unlikely event two crews have to man the *Columbiad* because we lose the *Vimāna*. We'd make it, but we would most likely have to shed about two thirds of the return samples."

"Then it means we still have a margin of one third the mass of the rocks."

Hugo nodded in agreement. He hadn't considered it in that way, but Komarov was: they still had some margin for this emergency plan.

"It took us 3 hours and 27 minutes to walk here, and 11% of our air reserves."

"Very good. Why are there three of you?"

"Oh..." said Aki, blushing, clearly understanding that she the unexpected addition to the group.

"I asked Aki to join us in order to get a photograph of all us, to send back to our homeworld."

Komarov gazed at Hugo without changing any expressions.

"To demonstrate how well we are getting along," continued a hesitant Hugo. Komarov was as tough to speak to as an indifferent audience. "I'm sorry I forgot to inform you."

Komarov grumbled and instead called out.

"Pande?"

An Indian man appeared behind Komarov, having just lowered himself from the ladder.

"Dr. Lange," continued Komarov, surprising Becky, since she hadn't introduced herself yet. Komarov clearly had deduced that if Aki was the unexpected addition, then that meant the third person was Becky Lange. "This is Pande, your counterpart. Please work out your exploration and experiment priorities. You can take photo before leaving," finished Komarov before he turned around and left them, still not inviting them inside his lander.

Aki was expecting to be able to ask everyone be included in the photograph, but Komarov was already climbing away.

Hugo had the same idea and he called out for Komarov.

"I'm sorry, Captain Komarov, we were hoping to have everyone be included in the picture?"

Komarov let go of the ladder and slowly 'fell' back to the airlock level, gracefully landing in front of them, thanks to the low gravity of Europa. But his eyes clearly showed he was in no mood to negotiate or be disturbed.

"Let me be clear," said Komarov. "Commander Iolienne's sacrifice to save our world from blackmail is why I am willing to sacrifice room on my ship. But that is all I need to sacrifice. Not my time or anything else."

Komarov restarted his trek up the ladder, having considered for a split second to just jump away, but understanding that would be seen derisively by the Westerners.

Hugo had a feeling they would not be meeting very often on the surface of Europa. They were even less likely to share tea.

Pande turned back around to face the trio, with a big smile. Becky was glad to see he was a little more sociable than his commanding officer.

Chapter 11

"I need to talk to the Discovery's engineer about the engine preparations" said Puff. "Which one of them is it?"

"It's *Otkrytiye* – not Discovery. And if you weren't bothered to learn their name, then I won't bother to tell you."

Puff jumped onto the seat next to the Commander.

"We could all *die* if you don't let me do those checks on the Ot-kree-tee-!" continued Puff in a sarcastic, childish tone.

"Would you have done them for the *Odyssey*?" replied the Commander without lifting his eyes from his private e-reader book.

"Of course not. The *Odyssey* is perfect. I designed the *Odyssey*'s engines."

"Then you don't need to worry about the *Otkrytiye*. Stop trying to get out of doing Becky's surface collection. I know she asked you to head for the Vernes rift and collect samples on the slope. Come on: chop, chop."

Puff let out a huge sigh of annoyance but took the ladder down to the EVA storage room. He was going to suit up, which was fine.

After hearing Puff moving around on the other level, the Commander had another thought:

"And don't you dare think about walking to the *Vimāna* to find the engineer. If I track you headed in the wrong direction, I'll ask the Russians to say they're all the engineers."

The Commander heard a loud box drop onto the floor. Clearly, he had foiled another plan.

Aki took advantage of this moment to secretly film the interaction. It would be a good addition to the variety of reports she had to send about the exploration. She had been doing the same work Puff was frustrated with. Becky Lange had assumed the mantle of "Collection Tsar", having to cram a year's worth of studies into three months.

Lange had been even more restricted when the quantity of samples they were supposed to take with them back to Earth was lowered in order to make more room for the fuel.

So she had decided not to waste time going out to various sites and taking time to dig. People not doing anything could do that work. Instead, Becky would focus on studying the samples brought back to her.

Everyone was doing their part, and for the most part, the unhappiest one was Becky. She loved her work – adored it. But not being the one doing the collection meant two problems existed.

First, she couldn't explore: she stayed at the *Columbiad* most of the time to execute the experiments sent to her by ISAF or that she came up with on her own.

Second: not everyone on Europa was very adept at doing the sampling, geological, and biological work. Becky sometimes found herself having to send someone back out to collect better information: was there dissolved silica at the base? Did they pyrolizer the sample? When they studied sulfur-containing thiophenes, did they do a spectrum analysis for butane or propane? Organic molecules were finicky. Becky knew that, but not necessarily a journalist, medical doctor or engineer. Although the medical doctor should still know a little bit.

Becky did take time to walk to the *Vimāna* to see her Indian counterpart and make sure they weren't overlapping studies.

Hugo insisted that two people go exploring the surface, even when it was to walk between the two landers, in pairs or more. The Indo-Russian crew didn't have such a rule, so the Indian biologist sometimes came over.

When Becky went, Ahmed accompanied her. He had his own studies to compare with the Russian and Indians at the *Vimāna*, which made the long walks fun.

Both Becky and Ahmed sometimes ran into language barriers when they were at the *Vimāna*. Becky knew it wasn't word wise, but expression wise. Sometimes, the Indians looked exasperated, while the Russians never smiled. Ever. Ahmed tried to make them laugh – sarcasm, jokes. Nothing worked. It did with Becky, she always laughed the entire walk home, but it didn't seem to be bridging gaps between the two spacecraft.

Becky was fortunate to be dealing with Pande, a warm, nice Indian man on the *Vimāna*, but the communication barrier still sometimes blocked. In the end, Becky thought using a radio would be just more effective, but she enjoyed the walks. There was good company.

It was a good break from the constant busy work. She knew that she'd have plenty of time to rest when they launched for Earth again and drowned herself in her work when aboard the *Columbiad*. But Ahmed often reminded her she still needed a break. It's like studying in college – half the work is knowing where to cut corners. "Look it up on Wikipedia," he would smile. He had a nice smile.

Becky sometimes relented, and would go for walks with Ahmed. Always to the *Vimāna*, to do official business, but in the back of her head, she knew that the time it took them to walk to the *Vimāna* was as long, if not longer, than sending a signal back to Earth and waiting for an answer. But she didn't care.

Throughout their time on the surface of the foreign, Jovian moon, Becky Lange didn't think much of her Earthly problems. She never really thought of Xavier or the kids. Only when they sent messages to her to say hello, but she usually just responded without thinking too much about it.

Europa was, ironically for her, the place where she could feel most like an Earth human: communicating with those immediately next to her. Going for walks. Looking at the magnificent planet-rise of Jupiter. Seeing the different striations of the Jovian clouds peek over the horizon, one by one... Timing them to see how much time it took. It was magical.

And she could share it with those that were on this other world with her.

Chapter 12

"Ok, guys," said the Commander over the intercom. "We've achieved a good orbit, we've got the *Otkrytiye* on radar and we're catching up to her nicely. We'll be docked in about sixteen hours. So let's get out of our suits and just sit tight."

The *Columbiad* booster engines cut-off right on time and the computer screens showed the spacecraft was on a good trajectory. To the untrained eye and ignoring the multitude of numbers around the screens, the circle representing Europa was encircled by a highly elliptical oval circling it. Which to the untrained eye would mean nothing other because it was an oval. What it meant they were not going to come crashing back down to the icy moon or into the enormous, windshield-filling gas giant that was Jupiter.

Just under 3 months having passed since they landed on Europa and 10 minutes since leaving it, the *Columbiad* was back in space with its crew. The launch had been surprisingly smooth. There was none of the shaking that they had felt in a simulator ride on Earth; the lack of atmosphere ensured that. Becky remembered the words from the first astronauts to launch from another world. Buzz Aldrin, during the Apollo 11 ascent from the Moon, had said it was a "very smooth...very quiet ride." He had also said something about being number 1 for take-off, which Xavier always thought was worth an eye-roll.

"How long before the Russians launch?" asked Lange.

"Another fifteen minutes. I just texted them to tell them that we're in a highly eccentric orbit and we'll be meeting up with the *Otkrytiye* as planned. I'm going to need one of you to sit with me for docking monitoring."

"Becky will do it," replied Puff from around one of the hatch doors.

"I'll handle it," answered Ahmed. "Becky and Olivia need to shift their rocks and plants around to prepare for the trip home."

Ahmed was right: the scientists all had to shift their research around to make more room for the return trip to Earth and to prepare for transfer to the *Otkrytiye*. The more things they could put in weightlessness at the center of the *Otkrytiye* meant there was more space available in the gravity-laden sections of the spacecraft. But for the launch, they had to leave everything where it was supposed to be. The engineers and mathematicians had planned their launch with precise weights and balancing. Any shift could have ended badly.

"When do you want me back here with you?" asked Ahmed. "Why do you even need someone?"

"We're docking two hours after our bed time: I need someone to make sure the readings make sense even if I'm sleep deprived. So I'll let you go to bed early to take a nap before meeting up with me at dock minus 10. So just be back at 0145."

"You got it, boss."

Ahmed floated down the hatch like everyone else had and headed back to his small bunk. He realized that everyone else had done the same. They all wanted to see the world they were leaving for the last time.

Looking out of the portholes, the entirety of the crew in the privacy of their own small, closet sized rooms watched the blue, icy world they were leaving behind. They were moving too slowly to see it shrink with the naked eye even if they were traveling at 20,000 miles per hour.

Without noticing it shrinking, Becky felt her feelings of accomplishment shrink. They had landed only 76 days before. It was only two weeks before they launched from the surface that she had really been able to get emotionally invested in her presence on Europa. They had barely had time to get used to moving around on the moon. There were so many secrets left behind, but in a sense, Becky was glad to be leaving them behind. They were heading back to Earth. Back to their families and true homes. It already had its fair share of secrets. Her two children growing up to be teenagers were going to make sure of that.

The feeling of sadness that came with leaving Europa wasn't so much an emotional attachment to the moon and the way of life the crew had grown use to, but simply a primitive, innate comfort of being on a large celestial body. Much larger than the cruise ship they were about to board for their return trip to home. When Becky was in her EVA suit and left the hab (however rarely that was), she had the whole world to explore. There was no risk of a gravity malfunction, or that the moon would suddenly change course or have an engine problem that could explode.

But the moon was locked around Jupiter. It wasn't going anywhere anytime soon. The only way it was bringing her closer to being home was by allowing time to pass.

Slowly.

"Ok boss," said Ahmed as he floated into his seat and attached his harness. "What do you need me to do?"

"Just sit here and make sure I don't miss anything that flashes red. And if I miss it, fix it."

"Sounds easy enough."

"The computers have it all. I'm going to bring up the blinds."

"Go ahead," agreed Ahmed.

The Commander flipped a switch and the small blackout blinds that covered the cockpit windows rolled open.

"There she is," muttered the Commander looking out the windows. "Our ride home."

"And we're right on time."

The two sat silently in their seats as they observed the computer screens that revealed nothing extraordinary. The training they had received allowed them to comprehend that they were about to dock with the massive starship outside their windows, which is what the Commander and Ahmed were primarily admiring.

It was a relief to see the ship, knowing that they were going to use it to head home. The Russians and Indians were not far behind them to dock with the *Otkrytiye*, but until then, the crew of the *Odyssey* would be docked but not enter the *Otkrytiye*. The Commander and Ahmed didn't think of that now though.

They observed the shape of the sister ship to their own departed *Odyssey*. It looked different from *Odyssey* even though it was oddly comparable. The two knew the engineering was almost exactly the same. Ahmed decided that it felt different because of the logos on the hull. The spacecraft had the Indian and Russian flags, along with the logo of the private corporation flying them. Whoever painted the ship used a different paint than was used by ISAF. And after an additional three months in space, the color probably faded more, as well. Some panel were missing; this was more aesthetically displeasing than an actual problem. Both astronauts knew that no critical systems were exposed. In fact, Puff would probably argue that it's better to not have the useless panels in order to facilitate moving into more critical nooks and crannies of the ship in an EVA suit.

"One kilometer..." started Ahmed.

"RALT Disagree acknowledged," interrupted the Commander, clicking a button that acknowledged the prompt that appeared in the bottom right hand corner of their screens. He then pressed a different switch while vocalizing his actions as was expected: "They're off because of the angle we're coming in from. It'll fix itself in a minute."

"Copy that. 900 meters."

The ship was firing its thrusters in an elegant ballet of synchronization. Automatically, lights from the hatch on the *Otkrytiye* lit up and lasers started to scan the *Odyssey*'s docking mechanism. A small green light signaled to the crew that the *Otkrytiye* agreed it could be docked with. If it had disagreed, the Commander could have still over-rode the system easily, but it would have been cause for pause and analysis.

"700 meters, closing rate 2.5 meters per second," commented Ahmed.

The Commander could read the data no problem, but Ahmed narrated it anyways to confirm he was reading the proper data and for posterity's sake. The data and voice lines were two separate systems that were broadcast back to Earth. Earth would be following the docking procedure, but if something went wrong and the data lines were down, then at least the data voiced by the crew would help the space agencies make sense of what went wrong. It was same concept as was used in black-boxes aboard aircraft around the world.

"Prox-ops program activated," announced the Commander.

"Hmmm," frowned Ahmed. "We stopped. Closing rate is 0."

A prompt appeared on the computer screens.

NAME MISMATCH
PROCEED? Y/N
WILL PROCEED IF NO INPUT IN 10... 9... 8...

"The *Otkrytiye* is broadcasting the wrong identification name to the *Columbiad*," announced the Commander. "*Columbiad* is thinking it should be docking with the *Odyssey*."

"Well that's not going to happen anytime soon," commented Ahmed.

"Nope, but we can proceed," agreed the Commander as he pressed "Y" and "ENTER".

The prompt went away and the closing rate between the two ships resumed.

"Why would the ship give you that countdown and continue to dock if there was a mismatch?"

"The *Otkrytiye* signaled a different name but still confirmed we could dock. *Columbiad* is programmed to understand that we could have been incapacitated during the launch and therefore needs to dock to whatever is out there, regardless of whether or not it was the ship we wanted."

"Of course, so that we can get the help we would need as soon as possible."

"Precisely."

Within the next minute, Lange was lightly shaken awake and heard the solid clamps latch onto the *Columbiad* and grasp the landing craft into the airlock socket. Lange tossed in her sleeping back and turned in her zero-G sleeping bag with a slight smile on her face before falling back asleep. They were docked with the spacecraft that could get them back to Earth.

"We have hard-dock," commented the Commander as he flipped a switch and ended the docking program. "Get on the horn with the Russians to tell them we've docked."

"Aye, Cap," replied Ahmed. "*Vimāna, Columbiad*, be advised we have hard-dock as of 0157."

"Understood, *Columbiad*. We will arrive in 15 minutes. We will advise when you are permitted to depressurize and proceed aboard *Otkrytiye*," came the reply.

"Copy that," replied Ahmed before switching off his microphone.

"We won't board until our morning, tomorrow," added the Commander. "The Russians and Indians are going to want to dock and get into their ship to make sure everything is good before welcoming us aboard. You wouldn't want to come back to your home and find someone already sleeping in your bed. We'll sleep here and tomorrow morning head into the *Otkrytiye*."

"I suppose not," agreed Ahmed. "So bed time?"

"Indeed. Thanks for your help. I've got it from here."

"Copy that," said Ahmed as he unfastened his harness and headed for his berth.

The Commander typed a quick message back to Earth announcing the good news.

Looking at the *Otkrytiye* through the windows of the *Columbiad*, the Commander suddenly felt a wave of anxiety flow over him momentarily.

"I wish you were here, Sophia," he muttered as he observed the off-color paint of the *Otkrytiye*, knowing it was all about to be very different for them tomorrow morning.

Taking a deep breath, the Commander headed for his own berth, hoping their adaption to life aboard the *Otkrytiye* wouldn't be too hard on morale. Missing life on Europa and adding strangers to their daily lives could have poisonous consequences, as Sophia had warned him. But she had also told him he was more than up for the task.

The Commander remembered that he could be in a worse position. He could be in Sophia's spot: three months away from impacting an asteroid spacecraft, alone in deep-space with no one to speak to live except for the automated ship-systems.

He typed Sophia a quick hello from his smartphone in his bed and allowed the *Columbiad* to broadcast the message to her.

How is your relationship with Siri? he also typed, in reference to an inside joke from an old TV series, The Big Bang Theory.

The Commander then shut off his lights and settled in for his first night docked to *Otkrytiye*.

"Pressure stable, ship is secure one," commented Aki.

"Open it," ordered the Commander.

Pressing the open button, Aki activated the mechanical switches that unlocked the heavy airlock and swung it upwards. The crew of the *Columbiad* simply floated and hovered there as they waited for the *Otkrytiye* to do the same and open their hatch.

They heard the latches on the *Otkrytiye* side unlock in a satisfyingly solid way and the door opened in the same manner, revealing the crew of the *Otkrytiye* also floating there, waiting to welcome their new crewmates.

It *looked* like the *Odyssey* did. But it didn't. It smelled different. It was just different, and instantly, Lange's feelings of loyalty to the *Odyssey* surged. Everyone's did. This wasn't their home, in their mind. This was the Russian and Indian home in space and they were just guests. Time would fix that perspective, of course, but right now, Lange and the rest of the *Odyssey* crew were simply not excited to be at the threshold of the *Otkrytiye*.

The interior colors were uncommon. Things were attached where aboard the *Odyssey* there would have been nothing hanging. The *Otkrytiye* was a modified copy of the *Odyssey*. The layout was familiar yet altered. It was like walking back into your home after having rented it for many years to someone else. Things were moved and changed. The smell of different spices wafted through the recycled air. The *Columbiad* was a small refuge in Becky's mind. She could always return to it if she needed to. But for most of their return to Earth, Lange and crew would have to spend time in the gravity sections of the spacecraft, which is where they were headed to now.

Lange presented a fake smile to her new crewmates. There was Gopal Pande, her Indian biologist counterpart; he still seemed excited to have a fellow biologist to nerd out with. They had cooperated on Europa to accelerate their experiments given their shortened stay on the moon. Of course, he didn't have to worry about learning how to use the bathroom aboard the *Otkrytiye*. He had been sharing it with his familiar crew all the entire way over. But even though the system would all be the same, Lange couldn't help but worry about the hygienic aspect of it. It was all so unfamiliar.

As Lange followed Pande down the corridor to the ladder that would take them down to the gravity sections, she thought back to her lessons about simple human feelings. She knew that her unease was simply caused because of her own habits. Habits were powerful and make people feel like their method of doing things was the best. These habits were familiar and *memorable*. That's why traditions continued. The American biologist knew that her feelings were a product of her unfamiliarity with the *Otkrytiye*. She would learn to love this ship, but many people who hated change would have been unable to adapt. On Earth, those people would have pushed for laws or legislation to prevent the change they feared: the habits that would have to be adapted. Or they would simply argue that the new ideas were dangerous to human kind. It wasn't just about things like homosexual marriage or the authorization to use stem-cells to cure diseases or repair damaged spinal cords. It went over things that today seemed like obvious decisions. Self-driving cars had to fight people who were convinced Humans were better. Two decades earlier, some pilots had tried to make the same argument when the autopilot aboard aircraft came to be but the technology was perfected to a point where passengers could tell when the autopilot was flying compared to the pilot – the pilot was never as smooth.

Change sometimes was offensive to some. It was misconstrued as a statement that their way was not as good as this method. Change required people to trust those who presented the next evolution. And trust was hard to give out.

After getting down the ladder into the dining room, Becky looked around and noticed there were two doors that were missing. Aboard the *Odyssey*, one door had led to the gym and the other to the play-room.

"How do you access the gym?" asked Hugo.

"We don't have a full wheel," replied Petrov, a Russian member of the *Otkrytiye* crew. "We have half the gravity modules your *Odyssey* has.

So if you want to go to another gravity section, you must go up to central node and float into another ladder corridor. Is this a problem?"

Oh boy.

Lange realized that this adaptation to change was going to take a while.

But like most change, they had no choice but to accept it.

"No problems," smiled Hugo.

He was about to introduce the rest of the crew but was interrupted by the Russian commander: Konstantin Komarov.

"We already know your names and professions, and some of you have already met on Europa. There is no need to do this again. You will all work together to transform Module 3 as living quarters. This will hopefully help us all get to learn about each other."

The groups proceeded to the 3rd gravity module and started to shift furniture around and transfer panels from the *Columbiad* to create a couple tiny rooms for the former crew of the *Odyssey*.

"So, which one of you is Korolev?" asked Puff after he put a box down. The fact that the *Otkrytiye* was still operating under Europan gravity made the move a lot easier than if they had sped up the ring to spin at speeds that would generate 1 G.

"Korolev is in engineering, monitoring and perfecting the engines."

"Monitoring and perf..." groaned an aghast Puff. "Ok! I'm going to head up there," replied Puff and he made a giant leap up the ladder shaft to head to the engineering section in the back. The low gravity allowed for some impressive theatrics.

"You guys might want to come see this," added Hugo to the other crewmembers. He had a feeling the encounter between the engineers, which had been avoided on Europa, could be a good opportunity to bond.

So the *Otkrytiye* crew and their new visitors aboard all floated quietly behind Puff and saw him call out for his Russian counterpart.

"Korolev? Korolev? Where are you at?"

A head popped out of a small crack in between two tanks, just in a section where the corridor was left off. Korolev's head was as a result, dark and looking at Puff's back as he continued to float back.

"Who calls me?" called out the head in a voice that surprised everyone.

Including Puff.

He grabbed a handle bar and stopped his forward motion and turned around to face the talking head.

"Korolev?"

"You will call me Dr. Korolev," said the cosmonaut as she floated toward Puff and revealed her face.

"You..." tried to retort Puff. "You... You're the... the engineer? But you're a girl?"

Lange slapped the back of Puff's head.

"You are not," replied Korolev with a deadpanned face.

"You didn't tell me this? You knew?!" asked Puff to his crewmates floating behind him in the long corridor.

"What should they have told you?"

"That you're the engineer."

"Would this make engines run better?"

That snapped Puff out of his surprise at the beautiful engineer hovering above him.

"What? No. They're prefect, and you should know that Korolev."

"Again, you will call me Dr. Korolev."

"You will call me, Puff. What did you say about the engines?"

"The engines are good. I've been able to make sure they're functioning."

"Good? Good? Are you serious?"

"I am always serious."

"No you can't be because you would know these engines are *perfect*. Perfect! And while your perfect body and gorgeous face are a distraction, you should still know that my engines are *also* perfect."

The other crewmates were all giggling at the interactions between the two. More at Puff's shocked expressions and frustrations at his Russian counterpart for clearly poking him and pushing his buttons.

Silently, another person floated behind all of them,

"Evrard?" grunted Komarov. "Everyone else, back to work."

Hugo looked up and noticed the Russian commander was clearly unhappy with the lack of work he had instructed earlier.

"Sorry, I just thought it would give the crew a little bit of a chuckle to..."

"You are aboard my ship now. Any issues, you either resolve amongst yourselves or I will correct them myself. I am in command and my commands are final. As far as I am concerned, you have been rescued from Europa and are our guests aboard: not crewmembers. My crew will have primary time in all laboratories, simulators and seats. What you do in your time, I don't care. Just don't touch anything."

Komarov floated away without giving Hugo an opportunity to say a word.

This was going to be an interesting year, but there was no choice, agreed Hugo. The Russian was in command and Hugo had been warned by Sophia about trying to usurp his leadership. All Hugo knew was that frustrations were about to skyrocket. The way the Russians and Indians did things would no doubt frustrate him and his crewmates. They would complain and moan, but hopefully it would stop at that. Hugo couldn't complain or even give a hint that he would support any sort of mutiny.

He felt it was going to be tough for him. Hugo knew he would naturally want to gravitate toward his crewmates and join in the blabbermouth chit-chat that was bound to arise and be a part of the team. But he couldn't allow that to happen – he had to show cool discipline. The storming phase between everyone was going to be dreadfully complicated. Seven nationalities and cultures meant someone was bound to say something like "that's not how it should be done, I know better." How that comment was handled would determine how difficult the storming would be.

Hugo had a new appreciation for those who sought peace: it was way tougher than just throwing a punch and hoping you win. Research had also shown that primitive instincts still drove some people to think that strength was raw power and violence. He worried about the Americans: they would want to prove superiority over everything from religions to culture and global power. He still remembered when the American astronaut Scott Kelly had returned from a trip to space that had lasted less than a year and was treated like a pioneer and hero. The reality was that the Soviets and Russians had already accomplished a feat. But it didn't matter: propaganda and a firm belief in exceptionalism (common for generations that did nothing to earn their privileges) meant Kelly was exceptional.

Thankfully, Becky Lange and even (surprisingly) Puff were level-headed Americans but Hugo still worried how far they could be pushed before his teammates snapped back something. He had left the nail gun on Europa without telling anyone. Hugo had confirmed with

ISAF and the Roscosmos that the same tool existed aboard the *Otkrytiye* just to make sure they still would have a tool, but didn't want to bring an extra one aboard that could be used as a weapon. Americans liked to live in fear. They still believed that life was not something to be shared between Humans, but to be taken (in case they felt remotely threatened). The arrogance had frustrated Aki when Hugo and she had spoken about guns once, and the American perspective of them. Aki had summed it up as supremely primitive and selfish. Aki couldn't understand how someone could warrant killing another; how they could believe they were worthier of life than a simple burglar (who was probably desperate in their life in order to warrant stealing). Hugo agreed with her and couldn't understand how people were so positively convinced that they would be the victims of a horrifying attack.

Becky originally could, since it was all over the news all the time, and in films, and of course, the "I have a friend of a friend" stories that for some reason made people believe that bad news was personal and therefore probable. Fear was a powerful tool.

Hugo knew he would not be using that tool to control his friends into complying with the Russians. No matter what happened, they had to get back to Earth and cooperation would be the best insurance. The first few months were probably going to be tough, but after that, the majority of the trip would be comfortable and nice. If someone became violent, it would ruin the trip forever.

For now, their wagon was hitched to the Russians and Indians.

Chapter 13

Deep inside the NSA floor known as the Node, Billy grabbed his Cinnamon Toast Roll Pop-Tarts from the microwave before heading back to his computer. His two computer monitors were placed in the middle of the row that had dozens of other monitor pairs and coworkers that were also lazily waiting for their own programs to execute.

Three flat screen televisions were mounted on the wall in front of all of them. The far left 32-inch screen had a live-stream of an asteroid. Hovering next to the asteroid, looking like a white knife stuck into a potato, was the ship threatening Earth: Dr. Montsegur's spacecraft. The images served as a constant reminder of why their work here at the NSA was so important. Fortunately, the other two monitors were more cheerful. The far right one showed the interior temperature and other stats of the supercomputers in an adjacent server room to which the dozens of monitors in the room were connected to. The middle screen was playing a DVD episode of House, MD.

The middle screen garnered the most attention from everyone in the room, as they were just there to make sure the code running in the background was running properly.

An email from Seohyun Choa just dropped in on his left monitor as his right monitor showed a DOS interface-looking program running lines and lines of code, following the stereotypical look of what a hacker computer looks like.

Choa was a Google engineer working in image recognition and artificial intelligence.

> Billy,
>
> Attached are the new parameters used for the Google Images search page. Backdoors and exploitable ports for the NSA to use are annotated. I provided the feedback you gave me about the PRISM algorithmic keys to the engineers, and they tried to make it fit, although some were perplexed by the dual-switch method you folks use to hack into HTML5 ports.
> We're trying =)
>
> Let me know if you guys need anything!
>
> Barring any feedback from you guys, it'll be live in 4 days.

Billy forwarded the email to his coworker, Thompson, sitting two computer stations down, enthralled in the television series playing on the TV screen. Once the email forwarded, Billy started typing away at his computer. He added the Google-provided code to the programs running searches across the Internet. Thompson would do the exact same thing as he was about to program, but on a separate server in order to minimize something being missed or a mistake being made. No single point of failure could be accepted in their work.

After a few minutes, Billy theatrically pressed 'enter' and then looked back up at the series. The little girl wasn't going to die after all – a happy ending to the 5th episode watched on shift.

Just like thousands of other stargazers around the world, Maria and James, a young Canadian couple, returned from their night-time observations.

After parking their distasteful Subaru, Maria grabbed the laptop case while James handled their heavy amateur telescope case.

Maria got inside and pulled out the USB key that held the images they had snapped with their telescope from the laptop-bag. James brought her a mug filled with warm tea as she turned on their desktop computer. After logging in, she plugged her USB key into the CPU tower.

Immediately, hundreds of lines of code started to run in the background. Since their computer was always connected to the Internet (why wouldn't it be), the images on the USB key were analyzed. The computer looked at the images of the pitch-black sky and the hundreds of white dots that showed different stars and other celestial objects.

Comparing the hundreds of images, the background-code saw a single dot was changing through all the frames. The dot was the size of a single pixel. Maria and James would never have noticed it. But the code was specifically programmed to see it. It also saw the other stars in the picture, the constellations and was able to determine where Maria and James had pointed their telescope.

Completing its analysis, the code terminated after executing a few commands.

All within the time it took for the icons on Maria's computer desktop to load.

Taking a sip of her tea, Maria waited for the computer to automatically open the folder showing the contents of her USB memory key.

0 items

She frowned and closed the window before maneuvering her mouse around the screen to open the window manually.

It still showed that there were 0 images and no data from the memory key that had been connected to their telescope.

"Oh no..." sighed Maria. "It looks like all the images are gone."

"What?" said James as he came next to her to look at the computer screen.

It was completely useless for him to be next to Maria to look at the same screen as her: it still showed a folder window open that had 0 items in it.

"Well it's a good thing we hadn't seen anything really interesting tonight."

The main door to the Node inside the NSA building opened. A gaggle of people flowed through, including Billy's replacement.

"Ready for change-over?" asked Billy's replacement.

"Yeah. New updated code from Google, Yahoo and Alibaba arrived and we processed it. Microsoft's update isn't in yet, I think they'll update in a few hours so that's really the only one you'll have to compile. Thompson and I got about 2,500 images off the Internet tonight...something like that. George and Katie topped 4,000."

"No shit? Well with that record to beat, I'll just give up now."

Billy chuckled as he grabbed his backpack that held a few books that he wasn't going to read unless the TV stopped working.

"Nothing else, buddy. The computers ran great tonight – no maintenance issues."

"Well I slept great knowing that a small patch of the sky was continuously being deleted from the Internet and hidden from the rest of the world."

"Indeed," agreed Billy. "All this to make sure no amateur astronomer sees the surprise we have for just one guy."

"Well that one guy being Montsegur...he did give us a hell of a surprise. It's only fitting we return the favor... Alright, get out of here."

He was referring to their work which was to delete any hint that the *Odyssey* was headed back to Earth – fast. Deleting any opportunities for someone to detect it was a top priority in addition to their second objective: keep Montsegur a secret from the world.

"I'll see you tomorrow bright and early."

"It'll be late for me."

"Touché," smiled Billy before leaving work after a long shift babysitting supercomputers that deleted a portion of the sky to prevent anyone from discovering the truth: a single man was holding the world hostage.

Even less likely to be detected, but still deleted from the planet's records was what the world was doing about it.

Chapter 14

"Ugh," sighed Puff. "Fine. Meet me back at the oil booster-pump latch at 19h00."

"Good," said Korolev as she floated back to the gravity-enabled sections.

Puff was pretending to be encumbered by the request, but deep down, he was thankful for Korolev and her 'demands'.

It had been about four weeks since they had departed Europa, and the excitement was still present. The astronauts still secretly re-watched various videos of jubilant crowds on Earth celebrating their landing. As far as the world was concerned, the astronauts were still on the Jovian moon, exploring the surface. A crevasse was being investigated by Hugo and Becky on the north side slope near where they landed.

But the only thing Becky was actually doing was re-watching a clip with Ahmed, on the spaceship quietly flying them back to Earth.

He made a comment about what his mother told him over a communiqué and Lange laughed. She covered her face with her hand as she laughed, comfortably sitting next to Ahmed on the loveseat in her pajamas.

Lange's phone vibrated, the universal signal the device had received a message.

A message from Xavier, but she suppressed frustration at the message and ignored it before returning to Ahmed.

It was the 14th message from Xavier she ignored.

"Check this out," said Ahmed showing something on his own phone's screen.

They giggled together like flirting teenagers. He pointed at something and she again chuckled, daring to rub her nose on his shoulder before pulling away. Ahmed didn't push her away. He simply also laughed, clearly showing how comfortable he was.

Over the PA, a call came.

"Ahmed, this is Hugo. Can you come over to the *Columbiad* for a second? I think there's a bad blue light sensor but I want you to take a look before I make the call."

Hugo didn't say anything and looked at Becky for a moment.

"Ahmed, are you there?" called out Hugo again.

"I'll be right over," said Ahmed. "Time to go save your skin," he smirked to Becky.

"Like you did at the Vernes chasm?" awkwardly flirted Becky. "Oh wait. I saved your butt on that one."

Ahmed was just as eye-rollingly awkward as he laughed almost too obviously, desperately trying to keep up Lange's seeming interest in him.

"I'll tell you what. Just one night. Let's do something neither of us have done in a very long time, and we won't speak of it again. At least, think about it," he smiled, with a resolve Becky found *so* attractive.

She tried to reason through her emotions. Becky was longing for human contact – intimacy. So was Ahmed, she knew. Her biological training was clear that sex drive was a powerful tool. Members aboard the ship were recommended by ISAF to masturbate at least once a week. That probably occurred more than once, given how she's had to monitor the different levels of strain the water-recycler had been under. Seven days had been the limit set by ISAF since that was the peak of serum testosterone driving libido in most humans.

The reality was that the body needed some of this contact suggested by Ahmed, and her feelings were tearing her up.

Pride, success, fame – all were pushing the crews to feel more brazen. Moral rules were already blurry on Earth with half the population disagreeing with the other half. In space, the only one making moral rules was the individual. Becky Lange in this case. Unless it was a universally disapproved action (like murder), no one had a claim to proper behavior. Cohabitation drove most of the crew's actions to stay proper and avoid frustrations. But she felt a different kind of frustration right now...

She felt butterflies when being with Ahmed. She felt happy and desired him. His body – the muscles along his back. She wanted to be held. To *feel* him.

Lange wanted the excitement. Not just the sex, but the feelings. The surge of adrenaline she had felt before walking on Europa. Before her first kiss with her first boyfriend. Or the other boyfriend. She wanted to hold her breath like she had when she saw the man she was interested in. Like she had when she had slept with Xavier for the first time. When she had received her astronaut badge. The endorphins flowing through her.

What was stopping her?

Lange knew deep down, nothing. It was only her inhibitions.

She was already tired of Xavier. The kids would never know and neither would Xavier, probably. She had just walked on Europa. On another world. She had explored the unexplored. She was traveling home on a foreign spacecraft while her Commander was going to save the world. Lange and her crew were sacrificing and risking so much to return on the *Otkrytiye*. She deserved this. It was just sex.

Korolev had already convinced Puff that she was perfectly able to make sex an event that was as benign as enjoying a cup of coffee with a friend.

Lange considered Ahmed's offer for a long moment.

Hugo was seething inside his cabin. Komarov, the commander of the *Otkrytiye*, was clearly playing favorites with the Indo-Russian crew and was keeping true to his word that the members of the *Odyssey* were just passengers and didn't have much access to the ship's systems.

The favoritism was *frustrating*. Hugo knew that it didn't really matter – all he had to do was just look out for his team and make sure they were doing ok. He knew they were doing ok right now, but he also was keeping the rumor secrets that others may not have heard. Komarov wasn't hiding to his Indian and Russian crew that the members of the *Odyssey* were not all that welcome aboard. Hugo knew that Komarov didn't hold to high esteem the crew of the *Odyssey*. At first, he understood why: he just needed to get to know the members of the *Odyssey* and things would improve. But Komarov did not care. He simply ignored whatever contributions the members of the *Odyssey* could bring and instead continued to run his ship as he had before.

Hugo knew this went against every leadership book he had read. The young man couldn't help but recognize that the lessons learned, though, were sometimes just not applied for the sake of personal preference or politics. Komarov was in charge, and things were going well for the members of his team, the ship was running fine, and the members of the *Odyssey* were only going to be aboard for a little while in the grand scheme of things. Careers weren't going to be destroyed, and this was an opportunity to do nothing.

And it was so *frustrating*.

These people selected for the space program weren't those that would easily sit down and do nothing. They had so many questions to answer from Europa and a hold full of samples that they could analyze. Hugo was fearing how the rest of his team was going to behave in a few weeks when the excitement of taking a break would wear down. When the boredom would settle in.

He would have to talk to Komarov. But right now, he had no political power. He was only the senior-most ranking member of the *Odyssey* team – but no accomplishments to show off to Komarov since they'd been together. Hugo's annoyance that politics had to exist even in such a remote place as here was enough to get him wanting to punch through a wall.

But he knew that would potentially tear a hole in the thin bulkheads of the ship and suck out the atmosphere and potentially kill all of them.

So he didn't.

Becky was still thinking.

The excitement of their achievements was fueling her justifications. She was successful, right now. That meant that she felt more permitted to do things morally questionable. Becky was a Europan explorer – she could do whatever she want. This feeling was empowering – freeing. Society was evolving all the time to move away from these restrictive, conservative mindsets. No one would care in a few decades, if anyone even still did.

But the end of the world could be around the corner. Did she want to be remembered as someone who broke her vow to her husband and potentially ruined a family?

The children wouldn't be affected at all, for once. They would be no evidence of her time with Ahmed. She and Ahmed were in outer space. There would be no visible change in behavior, different odors of perfume or anything that appeared as she came home.

If she ever got home.

Ahmed? Here and now.

Or Xavier? A promise for the future.

Or both?

What was one to do? Everyone had their own answer.

Chapter 15

The maintenance aboard the *Odyssey* was grueling sometimes, but there were advantages to being alone, decided Sophia.

It meant that all the tasks that were supposed to be split among the crew had to now be completely by a single individual: her.

The single occupant of the self-propelled space-station stayed busy. So busy she looked forward to the evenings, like any other western worker that toiled away in offices: the end of the work day.

Sophia knew that she could do whatever she wanted – she was the captain of the ship, the supreme commander and there was literally no one a million miles around that could tell her what to do.

"Well they could," she said out loud, "but they can't do anything about it."

The small SPHERE pod that floated next to her giving her the tools she requested continued to hover silently.

And Sophia continued to work as scheduled. ISAF had been clear in suggesting that she keep a constant schedule. For her sanity as she lived in total isolation.

An alarm started to ring.

It was the timer on her watch, signaling the end of the day.

Sophia didn't move though, except to silence the watch. She instead peeked back into the small alcove that had been revealed by removing a panel. She grabbed a three-inch metal clamp and latched into place.

The explorer then grabbed a wrench and tightened it.

"Alright," she sighed. "Reconnect fluid travel between... Alpha-8-0-9 and Alpha-8-1-1."

The SPHERE hovered there but Sophia knew the computer was processing the order thanks to a little amber LED on the tiny probe that blinked rapidly.

She picked up the small data pad that was behind her and saw the computer was slowly reopening the valves, allowing fluid to flow through.

She nervously glanced up at the work she had done, but it looked like there were no leaks. The computer displayed the PSIs within the system... 32%... 48%... 74%... 100%... 104%... 103%. It kept jumping between 104 and 103 percent, which Sophia knew was normal. The engineers had initially miscalibrated the sensor that measured the pressure in that section so the checklists and technical orders had been edited with the correct percentage number after launch. It had been the same thing with the Space Shuttles of old.

The main engines of the space shuttle had initially met 100% of their specification designed thrust. During engine development, the engineers had been able to meet the requirements, therefore, they met the thrust requirement at 100%. Later studies found that the engines could operate safely above 100%, as the engineers had insisted they could. NASA decided to not change the shuttle software information to re-peg the 100% mark in order to avoid confusion (100% thrust was also linked to other relationships to the engines, such as fuel consumption or pressure variations). Instead, they would just throttle up beyond 100%. The *Odyssey* now had a similar change, years after the last Space Shuttle returned from outer-space.

Puff always penciled in the checklists, next to the corrected numbers, that software engineers were not real engineers, and having to correct these things was the proof.

Sophia smirked thinking of Puff's behavior. As she replaced the panel, she knew that Puff would never have sent her an email or video-message, but Becky Lange and others from the crew probably did.

The lone occupant walked into the living room of the ship, ready to watch an episode of her favorite comedy show. She had her laptop sitting next to her, ready to go once the episode finished, but for now, these 20 minutes were going to be worry free. Seeing the characters interact, joke around and lead normal lives were what Sophia looked forward to the most every single day. It was the social interactions portrayed on the show that made her feel still a part of normal society – feel like she could also have friends like that. Regardless of how bad it got, she always had those episodes to cheer her up.

She plopped down on the couch and started eating her warm ration. Most of the food had supplies had been transferred to the *Columbiad* before it detached from the *Odyssey*. Becky had been a little frustrated that the additional weight meant fewer Europan samples could be carried home, but Sophia still remembered the simple answer to her frustration:

"Live or rocks: but you can't have both."

The threat of death from starvation was enough to convince Becky to let it go – the weight for food to take with them for the return journey was just more important.

Sophia still had a lot of work cut out in hydroponics to grow her food, but tonight was one of those nights where salads and other greens grown were not going to cut it. She just was feeling particularly lazy, and since she knew she had a couple rations to spare, she decided to use one tonight. Besides, she saved them specifically for these kinds of day, or for bad days.

Once the episode ended, Sophia wiped away her tears (Nick said he didn't believe in dinosaurs and his expression just made Sophia cry of laughter), and opened her laptop.

Because of the need for secrecy, the *Odyssey* only received messages from the *Otkrytiye* once a day through laser-link. That meant that if Becky or anyone else on the ship didn't respond to her emails before the due time, that she would have to wait another 24 hours.

But she didn't have to wait.

Sophia smiled when she saw a few emails from her former crewmates. According to Hugo, Puff was being occasionally bipolar: apparently the relationship he struck up with his Russian counterpart was a love-hate relationship. Korolev would criticize Puff's engineering, making him go ballistic, and then say they could have sex and he would be on cloud nine. Hugo suspected Korolev and the Russians were conducting some sort of psychological experiments with Puff and his behavior.

There were a few emails also from her homeworld: Earth. Her family was congratulating her for landing on Europa. They still thought she was on the moon, asking for a photograph with her visor up so that they could see her face. Sophia made a note that she was going to have to ask Hugo to send an old picture of Becky on Europa wearing the "Sophia Iolienne" name-tagged suit back to Earth. Sophia would only have to apologize to her family saying that the visor had to be on at all times, and any photos showing otherwise would very obviously get her in trouble.

Her last email to read was from Becky Lange. She clicked it open, and smiled as she read.

Becky had been reporting back, just like the others on what had been going on, but Sophia knew that she was also a release valve for all the pressure she had been holding inside.

There were days when Becky's emails were positive, seeming almost normal. But there were others where she just ranted – a lot. It was very detailed that Sophia sometimes felt guilty for enjoying those emails that were full of frustration. It allowed her to be a part of the team again. To be back with the ship.

Her mind wandered to why she couldn't be with her crew, able to help Becky. She didn't focus on why Becky preferred to email Sophia instead of her own husband (Becky had admitted as much in an email once), but instead on the culprit for all of this: Dr. Montsegur.

Sophia had spent a lot of time on the *Odyssey* (a lot) thinking about what his motives were.

In essence, she agreed with the man. It annoyed her beyond understanding that she felt that way. The man was holding the world hostage – there was no way to sugar coat this. She knew he was the evil, bad guy from another super-hero movie. But like in most well-made movies, Sophia also saw him as the tragic hero.

Dr. Montsegur's actions had already led to some significant reforms on Earth. The former commanding officer of the *Odyssey* knew that the Europan explorers were going to come home to a different world. One that saw even Russia comply with internal pressures. In a sense, he had helped vaporize the concepts of nationalism.

The background information provided about the hostage-taker determined he was very likely to follow through on his threat to release the asteroid to Earth if progress hadn't been made.

Any nation with nuclear weapons knew one thing about having them: threatening to use them had be credible, otherwise, no one would listen to you. Dr. Montsegur had credibility.

Credibility that he genuinely wanted to see a redistribution of wealth. Many pundits and commentators paid exhorbitant amount of money to pander to a base naturally called the man a communist fear-mongerer. Dr. Montsegur was clearly a Russo-Chinese agent trying to destroy our way of life.

Others saw him trying to promote a specific religion (even though he hadn't made any comments), when he had said that we had a responsibility to help each other. Dr. Montsegur had, in essence, ordered the invasion of some lawless areas of Africa. By the rest of the world. No more coalitions, or volunteer nations – everyone had to contribute. The UN budget had ballooned, much like ISAF's had.

ISAF: the organization that had inadvertently helped Dr. Montsegur. They had built the components, allowed the launches of his ship parts, but worse yet: demonstrated that international cooperation on a massive scale was possible.

Sophia shut her laptop lid, lost in thought. The complexities of unifying the world were astonishing. No magic wand, or rock, could change that. But Dr. Montsegur had made it no secret that he wanted to be destroyed. He also was certain that the only way that would happen would be through a concerted, unified world effort.

Sophia sighed at how disappointed he was going to be. Instead, the plan called for one space object to crash into another one. Earth wasn't even going to be bothered with this.

Dr. Montsegur's intent was good. But misguided. He was taking aim at the people the world already wanted to eradicate: bigots, self-centered fearists, those that still wanted to live in clans. But with his asteroid, he was using the proverbial sledge-hammer to hit a tiny nail.

Sophia just hoped she got to change his misguided ways before it was too late.

In the meantime, she would respond to Becky Lange, who lived in a somewhat more isolated world than Sophia did. While Sophia was alone aboard the *Odyssey*, she was not subjugated to isolation by her fellow crewmates (since she didn't have any). That would have made her feel worse than being actually alone, and she could easily empathize with Becky's sentiments.

Hugo was doing his best to help the crew, but Sophia knew that the situation was not ideal. Having people become ever more reclusive could lead them to missing out on opportunities. Or feel even more depressed – sequestered from the community they were supposed to be a part of. Bitter and resentful.

These were feelings that Sophia wanted to help Becky overcame. And then evade.

So far, I'm doing a pretty good job... she thought. *Nope. No, I'm not,* she corrected herself.

Chapter 16

Three months.

Not even that much.

Becky sighed as she looked at herself in the mirror. It had almost been only three months since they had left the surface of Europa. It definitely felt like a lot longer than that.

These hadn't been easy.

Lange tried not to think about it, but the reality was that if Sophia didn't manage to take out Dr. Montsegur's asteroid-latching spacecraft, the next three months aboard the *Otkrytiye* were not going to matter. Life on Earth would be chaotic and unpredictable. If life even survived. The asteroid would cause global devastation on a scale never seen in Human history. Lange's only hopes laid with Sophia and the capabilities for Human technology to help the species adapt and live in even the most extreme environments.

The crew only had each other to get through those dark thoughts. Inhabitants of Earth found out recently about the pending threat over their minds, but many ignored it. There wasn't anything they could do about it. Only national leaders could. It apparently was oddly reminiscent of the Cold War era when a nuclear apocalypse was something to be expected. People had to trust the government would watch out for them.

The planet finding out about the looming asteroid that could be lobbed at them didn't mean they were permitted to learn about the ace up ISAF's sleeve to fix the problem. That would most likely mean Dr.

Montsegur would not find out as well. So as far as Earth knew, the Europa mission was just about to take-off from Europa. As far as the world was concerned, the crew of the *Otkrytiye* landed on Europa first. Sophia was still in command of the crew of the *Odyssey*, and the pre-recorded videos were proof enough of that. They resolved her not being seen on the videos of their first steps on Europa by simply saying that someone had to be holding the camera. ISAF was just thankful there were hardly any photographs of Neil Armstrong on the Moon. The first man on another world had very little proof of being on the Moon yet no one (except for the occasional paranoiac) doubted he had been there. So Sophia was holding the camera and for subsequent shots, Ahmed and Aki took turns going out in Sophia's suit to get pictures of her nametag outside the spacecraft.

With all these lies (because that's what they were, regardless of how you tried to frame deception), Becky was alone. The fact that she was headed home early was lost on her husband and children. It had been a year and a half since they had been able to speak to her live. Life had moved on. The children were busy with children things, and Xavier was busy with them and didn't focus on Becky's mission anymore. Now that Becky was aboard the *Otkrytiye*, the Russians controlled the mission. Xavier was working in the hush hush world that was the *Odyssey*'s new mission so he didn't brief too much to her. The tone coming from the video recordings made it sound like the recordings were chores more than anything. The kids looked like they were forced to send a hello message instead of being able to play.

Becky knew it was the same from her side. She missed her kids terribly, and sometimes ended up crying silently in the privacy of her room. But there was nothing to do nor talk about. Her messages to her family were lethargic as well. She had nothing to report. She had a few small envelopes from Xavier that she had yet to open. Becky considered opening one now. After all, she had been saving them for when she would feel this way. She hesitated and decided to readdress that idea later. Her husband had written her multiple notes like these to remind her that he did care for her, even if the challenges of travelling so far would make her forget it.

With the excitement of Europa gone and the interminable wait to return to Earth now prevalent, the crew was bored. The only source of excitement would come from whether or not the *Odyssey* would succeed in its mission to destroy its sister ship in a collision. But not even they were privy to the information on whether or not the new mission was on track; they had no reason to know, so they wouldn't.

In an odd sensation, Lange knew that her trip to Europa could result in her never seeing her children again. She had known the risks: something could go wrong and kill her at multiple stages of the mission. Xavier and many others had pointed out that she still had higher chances of dying in a car accident or something else unexpected. It was impossible to predict. Nevertheless, even knowing she could never see her children again, Lange had trouble staying sane with the knowledge that Dr. Montsegur and his asteroid could kill her in family in an instant. She would never see them again, but it wouldn't be because of her own death. She would have to watch them die.

Becky Lange came to the realization of what she had put her family and friends through when she accepted the Europa slot. It was easy to self-sacrifice. The tough part for them was that they had to watch their friend die.

The worse part was that Lange knew she should feel like she missed them. She knew she should miss Xavier; She should want – yearn! – to talk to him.

She didn't. Lange dreaded talking to Xavier – she didn't want to hear about his day. About what was going on his life, what things made him feel happy or sad. Hearing those words was like listening to nails on a chalk board. It only fueled her annoyance with her husband.

As far as the astronaut was concerned, she had her life here in space now. She had no desire to be reunited with her loved ones. Rationally, she kept telling herself to wait before just jumping to such a conclusion. Wait until she returned to Earth. In the meantime, she would just live her routine.

The routines were evident across the entire ship. Hugo had managed to convince his Russian counterpart to allow the crew of the former *Odyssey* to keep busy with the *Otkrytiye* up-keep. It wasn't the experiments he was hoping for, but fixing the ship was in everyone's interest and it kept them busy. *Small victories*, thought Hugo.

The ship was running far better than was originally planned in some areas, and was falling apart in others. The interplanetary starship had double the crew it was intended which meant double the attention on its engines, its wiring, piping. And double the toll on its water and oxygen filtration systems. The *Columbiad* was helping and the engineers of the ship had been savvy enough to allow the sharing of all piping and systems with the mothership *Otkrytiye* (probably as a result of the Apollo 13 mission when the Command Module and Lunar Module CO_2 canisters were incompatible, almost killing the crew until NASA figured out a way to literally make a square peg fit into a round hole.)

But the water filtration systems were being used in zero-G the majority of the time aboard the *Columbiad*, which hadn't been planned. Fortunately, the engineers built the *Columbiad* with levels of resiliency that meant only a little light maintenance was needed.

Unfortunately, the engineers aboard the ship found out that some of their Earth-bound counterparts had cut corners in the development of the *Otkrytiye*. While the designs were similar, the materials in some sections were substituted. The million-dollar toilet that was often mocked by Earthlings was in fact not supposed to be any cheaper, because otherwise the various stresses applied to it through different accelerations and masses applying pressure, cracks could appear. This was also evident to Puff, Olivia and Hugo as they continued with their Russian and Indian teammates to repair the *Otkrytiye* in the same spots over and over again.

It was tedious. The same problems over and over again. Hugo knew they had to remain vigilant and tried to take the lead in most of the repairs he could handle, but then he still had to deal with the daily concerns brought up by his crew; or more significantly, not brought up.

The evening dinners they used to enjoy were gone. Access to the dining room was not officially restricted, but the Orientals had made sure that their food stuffs, spices and other odor-generating items created a waft that meant no one from the *Odyssey* would be confused with which access shaft led down to the dining room.

The crew just wasn't interested in bonding anyways. They were bored, isolated... which led to apathy and simply unhappiness. Their excitement for the mission was replaced with resignation. They were guests aboard a ship that wasn't theirs. Earth had moved on from the successful Europa landing to more pressing issues such as 'jobs.'

Whereas everyone would talk about each other's families or friends, the existence of such family and friends was now put into doubt. No one ever spoke to each other anymore, except in hushed 'hey's' as they passed each other. Sophia had urged Hugo through her latest email to forcibly try and have a small talk with everyone on the crew once in a while. Hugo was uncomfortable with the idea of playing ships' psychologist, but it was his responsibility as their leader. He needed them to keep up their efforts and not sink into despair because of the isolation they were suffering from.

He had spoken to Aki first, which he knew would be the easiest. The perky Japanese astronaut always had an ability to adapt in isolation and had already been isolated culturally from the majority of the crew since the beginning. As communications officer, she also didn't communicate a whole lot. But her drawings were still a hit, which was the source of Hugo's first idea of many to help reboot morale aboard the *Otkrytiye*.

The biggest hits were sarcastic drawings of the tensions between the Eastern and Western crews – she had a unique perspective of how ridiculous the tensions could be sometimes. The Japanese scientist knew that food from the Indians had a different odor, but so did American foodstuffs. She had to adapt and remembered going through the same process, although she hadn't had to learn while travelling between planets. She vented her tensions through the drawings and it made others laugh, also lowering tensions. Some crew-members had even gone to her to ask for a drawing that could communicate a frustration. The drawing would bring the problem to light and hopefully rectify it.

If it didn't, her second de-stressor would come in: MarioKart.

The bubbly characters and colorful worlds allowed for the entire crew to blow steam. Of course, some astronauts, smart as they were, sometimes forgot that no matter how hard they pressed the accelerate button, the kart didn't go any faster. New signs across the ship were drawn on the walls: "Blue-Shell Free Zone" next to the tunnel, while "Caution – Slippery – Bananas Present" had been drawn in the kitchen area.

Apart from those few moments of social connection, though, everyone kept to themselves.

Every day.

Every night.

Day after day.

After day.

The leader of the *Odyssey* team was dedicated to getting everyone talking to each other again, instead of remaining in their small two-person groups that then secluded the rest of the crew. Hugo still had tried to talk to Lange next, but it was more of a lesson in how awkward a conversation can be.

"How's Xavier?"

"Fine, sounds like they're doing well on Earth."

"Good. And the kids are doing well?"

"I suppose. According to the report cards, they're doing great and making friends."

"Ok... Any new dishes you've tried to cook here?"

"No. You know who cooks meals every evening."

"Right... Are you doing ok?"

"You know I'm all for a good psych-eval from time to time, but is this really the time, Hugo?"

"When would be a good time?"

"I don't know, not now?"

"Well you have to admit everyone is a little down."

"Yeah but what do you expect? We're just floating through space here, no one here or on Earth cares, and we're just waiting a real long time for our lives to start again, that's if they ever even start again since there's an asteroid threatening to hit the planet."

"So the solution is simply to just no longer care about anything?"

"You make it sound so depressing, but what's the harm in just sitting and taking a break? Our whole lives, everyday preparing for this mission, it was just go-go-go. You'd think they would have prepared us for this."

Hugo nodded in agreement. The flight training had not included extended periods of sitting and waiting, or having to work with other crew members you weren't screened to work with. This was uncharted territory, both in space and in human interactions. The meticulous decades of analysis, of lessons-learned, planning for every eventuality had broken down. ISAF was going crazy on Earth, but there was nothing they could really do about it. Isolation just hadn't been a plan. Hugo had lived through that.

"You know, I spent a year at the South Pole."

"I think I did know that. A while back, right?"

"Yeah, we don't need to say how long back."

"At the actual South Pole or just somewhere in Antarctica and you round to South Pole like those American airmen at Thule Airbase in Greenland round their location to 'North Pole'?"

Hugo laughed: "No, I was at the actual South Pole. At the Amundsen Scott station."

"And then you thought: I need more ice. I should go to Europa."

"Pretty much," chuckled Hugo. "But there were times at the South Pole that things got pretty rough, and we weren't really all that bored. Do you know why it was tough?"

"I don't know, Hugo. Missing family, no McDonald's, too many penguins?"

"No, it was because of the darkness."

Lange frowned at the unexpected answer.

"It was completely dark for about four full months in a row," continued Hugo. "We all handled it in different ways, but the bottom line is that, as you must already know being a biologist, we're a mammalian species that evolved working daily with sunlight. When we don't have it, we start changing our behaviors and the first thing that can be affected for some is their motivation."

Lange took a deep breath before giving him a polite smile.

"Well thankfully we're not at the South Pole in total darkness. We're in a spaceship that's constantly bathed in sunlight."

"That wasn't really my point."

"I know," she fake smiled. "Sorry, but I need to go check on the crops in the hydroponics lab."

Hugo sighed and watched her leave. The astronaut had noticed some of the crew-members from both sides just create their own little cliques, but each group never bonded with another. It was like an oil and water reaction.

Lange and Ahmed had often been found spending some time in the same cupola reading or sharing a meal. Whenever they were together was the only time Hugo saw them smile; it was in fact, the only time anyone ever caught a glimpse of a smiling Lange.

Puff and Korolev had made no secret of their new sexual relation although they hid in one of the engine manifold node compartments where no one else ever even came close. Hugo knew that it wasn't going to become a real relationship and wasn't too concerned about it. Puff was married to his engines (no pun intended). All Korolev had to do was remind him that the engines were malfunctioning and he would be running laps around the ship in frustration of her ignorance concerning the majesty of the interplanetary drive.

As Hugo knew, this was their post-landing depression phase.

Everyone was growing tired of the Russian commander and the clear preference the Russians and Indians received from him. Hugo felt like the rest of the crew that had been on the *Odyssey* viewed him as useless.

Puff certainly didn't care about listening to him without some fine nudging.

The simple reality for the crew at this stage of the mission for the former *Odyssey* members was that they just accepted being relegated as second-rate astronauts.

The circle of preference was frustrating for the first few months – Becky and the rest of the crew were trying to write papers to show they could contribute to the mission and development of the scientific conversation. Puff had to sneak into the engine bays to execute fixes he knew needed to be done, but it didn't help him. The Russian commander only saw the ship running smoothly and continued to assume that it was his engineer doing her job. The crew worked hard to feel like a part of the team and accepted. To feel valued.

But they weren't.

Instead, the Russians and Indians kept true to their word: they were rescuers and the others just had to sit tight until they returned to Earth. Komarov, the ship commander, kept on trying to say it was to prevent putting too much of a burden on a grieving *Odyssey* crew, but that wasn't true. He simply failed to understand that so far from family, in an isolated community, they couldn't be boxed into even smaller boxes. Creating clans could lead to 'them-vs-us' mindsets, only enflaming the tensions.

Hugo was fighting tooth and nail to prevent that. He could never accept any individual favors from Komarov for fear that it would make him look like a favored member. If anything was going to be given to Hugo, it had to apply to the rest of the members of the *Odyssey*.

But even he was starting to give up.

The isolation was also taking its toll. There were days where everything was fine and he was optimistic about the whole mission, even if he didn't have much to do with it. He was a still a part of it.

But like the rest of his crew, there were also days when he was just frustrated and angry. These swings were unpredictable – it didn't matter which side of the bunk he woke up on, or how many hours of sleep he got. One wrong word or policy mention from one of the Indo-Russian goons could annoy Hugo. Or someone from his crew, which would also have to be dealt with.

They only had a few months left aboard. The ISAF commander seriously considered just acting as a liaison officer to the rest of the crew and spending time with Aki playing MarioKart or learning how to cook with Becky and Ahmed in the *Columbiad* kitchenette.

The kitchenette!

Lange was reading when Hugo interrupted her and suggested an idea.

Two days later, they were ready to unveil the surprise, and they invited the crew of the *Otkrytiye* to partake.

Aki floated down into the ship's living room. The lights were off. As she flipped on the switch, the crew shouted "SURPRISE!"

Aki jumped in complete terror before her brain caught up and she started to laugh and smile.

"Happy birthday!" said various crew members as they gave her hugs or shook her hand.

"Oh" smiled.

"So how old are you?" asked one of the Indian crew-members.

Aki made an 'oh' look, as if she were in trouble, then covered her mouth smiling. She wouldn't say.

"For once I'm not the moron asking a stupid question," smiled Puff as he ate a biscuit.

The rest of the crew laughed.

This was her third birthday with the crew, but her first with the crew of the *Otkrytiye*. Like last time, they put on stereotypical anime films, while Becky had used a boom-box to play K-Pop and J-Pop music in the long central tunnel for weightless dancing. This was the first time members of the *Otkrytiye* crew had tried dancing in a weightless environment. The results made them all laugh, seeing each other 'dance', but Puff described it more akin to looking at frogs trying to swim in air.

And they offered Aki a tiny cupcake that Hugo and Becky had made a few days earlier from some of the chemical elements they had and food rations they had transferred from the *Odyssey* many months ago.

This was one of the good days. Hopefully, they would last to the end of their journey.

Chapter 17

Sophia was lucky being by herself aboard the *Odyssey* at this point.

"Houston this is *Odyssey*, ready for gyro activation for plane reset and zero bubble – Ah…roger, you're cleared zero bubble. – Wow thank you, ISAF, you guys are really swell," babbled the astronaut to herself as she pressed two switches next to her inside the Flight Deck of the massive starship.

Giant gyroscopes started to whirr outside the spacecraft, slightly adjusting the pitch of the spacecraft by a few degrees as it continued its arced trajectory through the solar system.

A few seconds later, a faint beep announced the receipt of a data package from the *Otkrytiye*.

The sole human aboard the *Odyssey* knew that she would seem crazy to anyone else who saw her talking to herself. The astronaut excused it by remembering that most people talked to themselves when alone in their own homes or cars.

The *Odyssey* had been her home for the past two years, and hers alone for the last year of the two. Sophia had tried to entertain a conversation with Leonardo, the SPHERE, even considering to rename the little robot Wilson, but finally relented. The software didn't have an option to change the name without changing a hundred other parameters. Sophia's laziness had gotten the better of her and she decided it was better for her to have a ball to talk to with an original name, instead of renaming it after an inanimate character from a film starring Tom Hanks.

Opening the data package, she selected various menus on the computer to have it run on only one of the five computers first. If there was a problem with the code, it wouldn't affect the entire ship but only the test computer.

While the lines of code ran, Sophia opened on another screen the graphic representation of the program. She could read the ridiculous computer code that was a separate language on its own (like C+, Python, Basic, Fortran) but she preferred having a computer translate to pictures, graphs and icons.

It was another set of course corrections. Two hours away from her target, she saw a red line showing her old trajectory and the blue line showed her new one. It was off by a few tenths of a degree, but with the distances involved, it could mean the difference between hitting her target or flying so far next to it that her ship would look like a speck of dust.

Analysis from Earth ground-based radars also revealed what orientation the target spacecraft had which meant adjusting the velocity in order to guarantee the whole reason why Sophia had been alone for the past year was obliterated.

Strapping into the commander's seat on the Flight Deck, she fastened her harness. It wasn't because of a risk of a crash, but simply because in space, when floating if the vibrations threw her to the left, it would take a lot of effort for her to move back to the right. On Earth, gravity allowed that motion to be predictable and manageable, but in space, Sophia knew that if she wanted to be able to reach switches around her for whatever reason, she couldn't be floating and buffeted around because of vibrations caused by the burn.

She closed a guarded switch, that did something only an astronaut would understand, flipped another switch that dimmed all the lights across the ship to limit the electrical load demanded, and then connected the other computers when the first one agreed the new program wasn't corrupt.

Unlike in movies where operators always flipped switches all around them, she simply opened the program again when all the computers were synched and started the program. In a few minutes the *Odyssey* would be in a position in space that was where the calculations had been planned for a change in correction. Fuel parameters, thrust times and burn times were all planned on the spacecraft beginning its maneuver at that point in the universe. When the spacecraft would detect it had arrived at that point through its starlight sensors, then it would ask Sophia if she wanted to continue. No need to flip fifty switches for the sake of drama.

INITIATE TRAJECTORY CORRECTION PROCEDURE? Y/N
    Y

The *Odyssey* had a soft rumble emanate throughout its compartments as the primary engines which was surprisingly reassuring to Sophia. It felt normal – like any other burn she had experienced in the past two years.

A new message popped up on the screen at the end of the burn, which Sophia thought was surprising. She wasn't expecting anything again for a little while.

Commander Iolienne –

Sophia, you are now inside the window where even if Dr. Montsegur detects you, our communications or your engine radiation signature, he will not be able to achieve enough velocity for the asteroid to be a threat to Earth. ISAF will now uplink other sensor telemetry to the Odyssey for terminal course adjustments.

We have the Phaeacian on the launch pad prepped and ready to launch the moment we confirm through sensor coverage that the threat to Earth has been eliminated. It should arrive at your crash position about 5 + 25 hours after launch, so you should have plenty of oxygen to spare in your space-suit by the time rescue reaches you.

"That's very nice, but that's all contingent on me not dying *in* the crash," said Sophia before continuing to read the message.

We are right now claiming to the media that the Phaeacian being rolled out to a launch pad is for tests and inspections for the returning Europa crew. It will fly out to you and adjust the course of the asteroid as need be to ensure it's never a threat to Earth again.

Humanity owes you a debt of gratitude.

As you mentioned through other communiques, this message will not include any mushy good-byes. ISAF is proud of you, and thanks you. Your parents are proud of you and will always love you. Mr. T. Dreke says he loves you and will be thinking of you, always.

You may send your own notes up until expected loss of signal.

Joe Augustine

203009211318Z//JA//1318Z

"Well...thanks, Joe," sighed Sophia. "Now ISAF will be able to talk to me directly and tell me how terribly I'm doing things."

She checked the schedule of events again and noticed that she had about an hour before the terminal phase would begin.

The Commander didn't need to be in the seat in order to 'fly' the spacecraft, only to monitor it and override commands. The ship was a marvel of sophistication, similar to the Apollo spacecraft that landed on the Moon. So long as you are willing to follow the laws of physics, spaceflight can be relatively easy and only depends on the proper timing of your maneuvers. Which fortunately for Sophia, wasn't up to her but a series of well-programmed computers that *definitely* processed information faster than she did.

It was unfortunate that that relative ease of space-flight that made it possible for her to have to do what she was going to do today. Dr. Montsegur had clearly figured out a way to gain the upper hand on the entire world, including the powers once thought to be invincible, such as the United States...or Russia...or China...or France...or the United Kingdom. And their nuclear arsenals. All through a couple of well timed-thrusts and Newtonian physics.

"This is Commander Sophia Iolienne aboard the *Odyssey*, recording the final moments prior to the deliberate collision between the *Odyssey* and Dr. Montsegur's ship. This record is intended to provide an account of the upcoming events, a tool to investigate the sequence of events, and I suppose also a piece of posterity since I'm probably not going to get off this machine alive, given that part of the solution to stop Dr. Montsegur is to allow the reactor aboard the *Odyssey* to go boom. Just in case though, I'm in a spacesuit, if anything so that if I'm ever found I don't look *completely* terrible. I know that the spacecraft pod I'm sitting in was designed to survive a reactor explosion but given that there may be two reactors exploding – when you include his, I don't expect this to hold in one piece. I've linked the computer data lines of code to another redundant copy of records just to be safe and it's being saved to a separate wireless USB drive that I am holding in my pocket right now. If you want it, come find me," she said in a sarcastically voiced taunt. "With that said, preparing for helium disk bursts and coolant pipe shut off."

A few minutes later.

"I've confirmed the coolant pipe shut-off and already severed the redundant link so the reactor is no longer receiving any coolant fluid. I've got about 12 minutes until the automatic ignition for the MC-17-09-21+24 burn which, by god, will henceforth be called *the* burn," sighed Sophia. "I'm going to recycle the RTCC just to make sure we have a steady flow into the JKLOL... Ridiculous acronyms now that I think of it. But I won't stop! RCS's checked out good, as expected... So, I will be back. I will be out of range of the data-relay so there might be a gap in the data coverage. It would really suck if something terrible happens while I'm down the tunnel. Oh well."

"Ok," said the commander as she got back to her seat in the Flight Deck. "Alright, the back checked all-good so I'm going to run the pre-burn checklist... For *every – single – crew-position*, covering for a crew that is not here with me.

UHF radio – power panel switches – N/A

APU Panel – Bleed air valve set to close, generator to ON, cleared – check.

AC Bus Tie – ON. I see AC off light extinguished, and AC Bus tie SW ON light is illuminated.

AC Bus Tie switch to OFF... I see AC off light is now illuminated and the AC bus tie SW ON light is extinguished. AC Bus Tie checked.

Bleed Air System... divider valve switch to CLOSED, APU bleed switch to OPEN, Bleed Air System – checked. Oh look, a Caution is associated with this step."

Sophia remembered back to her countless hours of flight and space training. Whenever operating heavy machinery, there were three annotations every crew-member had to be aware of: Note, Caution and Warning. She again recited to herself some facts as she ran through a checklist for the Omni-bus maintenance.

"A Note is an operating procedure, condition or statement which much be highlighted. A Caution highlights an essential operating procedure, condition or statement which, if not strictly observed, could result in damage to, or destruction of equipment, or loss of mission effectiveness. – Oh wow, Sophia. Tell me what Warning is then. – Well let me tell you. A Warning highlights an essential operating procedure, condition or statement which, if not strictly observed, could result in injury, long-term health hazards, or death. – Jeesh, Sophia. That sounds intense. – You're right. Pretty much everything on this ship needs a warning label since a damaged or destroyed piece of equipment could mean death."

A beep interrupted Sophia. *Another* message?

NEW TIMELINE CORRECTION. MOVED TO LEFT 30 MINUTES.

"Uh oh," said Sophia. "You'll be happy to know that the fate of the world just shifted 30 minutes earlier. I have a feeling someone did some bad math. Which means I only have 10 minutes to run through this checklist. So let's accelerate this."

She flipped a switch to bring up another menu for the most important checks she thought were relevant: reactor and RCS.

"Reactor pressure regulator to OFF... Manifold check...drop, light. Drop from 30 to 15 psi checks out....at 12 seconds. In tolerances.
Inverters to DC bus – SET.
TIT checked – 970.
Hydraulic pump switch to ON, flap lever to OPEN.
Auxiliary pump switch to STANDBY – AUTO FAILOVER.
Electrical gyros governors set to OFF. That's a deviation from the checklist but I don't need the gyros to work past this maneuver so governors stay off.
Checking electrical connections for Power Panel 1 – no red lights on screen so I'm going to assume that means SDCs 1, 3 and 5 are all good. I'm not going to check manually. Screen for Power Panel 2 shows SDCs 2, 4 and 6 also shows no red, moving on.
OF/OA radar activation..."

Sophia paused for a moment and decided that she should warn ISAF that she was about to start using that Obstacle Finding/Obstacle Avoidance radar. It had been turned off for the past few (more than that) days to prevent detection from Dr. Montsegur given that it was like a giant 'I'm here' device that radiated so much energy it could easily be detected. She needed to reactivate it for the new trajectory correction code that was sent to her. ISAF knew she'd have to turn it back on, but hopefully they didn't expect her to do it later, because she was doing it now.

"ISAF, *Odyssey*, be advised, activating OF/OA."

There! The message was simple enough that ISAF wouldn't be surprised if Dr. Montsegur saw it but it was still cryptic enough that he wouldn't suspect a thing yet.

"Back to business because I have...gods – 5 minutes to main engine ignition.

BMAP selected.

EXP – OFF

FREQ set to X2... I'm setting it to X3 to try and blind it as much as possible, since my goal here is to not avoid an obstacle...

REGR MODE – A-XK.

BCN declutter selected.

ISO ECHO – OFF.

Antenna tilt - SLAVED

Roll cancellation program – OVERRIDE...

Come on..." muttered Sophia waiting for the computer to load the data.

"I see the first sweep," she said soon after.

On the screen dedicated to the radar technologies, she saw the device warm up and the proper data loading.

"Finally! Ok,

No checking the TST link.

E2 Switch – SELECTED, radar activated.

M-Ku, REGR MODE checked out.

OA selected – I'm on 800 NM and I see colors – checked.

PGM selected and checked.

Mission Computer links are MC 1 and 4, MC 2, 3 and 5 on hot-standby.

ISAF hack for OF/OA program adjustment activated... And running."

On the screen, a series of lines of code started to flow. The computers were being taught to track toward the object instead of automatically avoiding it.

It would have been too complicated to rewrite the entire operating system of the *Odyssey*, so she would have to manually override conflicting demands from the ship. The spacecraft would move toward a single point in space where they suspected the target was.

As the *Odyssey* was getting closer, the radar was needed to find exactly where their target was... Using a radar that was designed to avoid things. It was a conflict of interest that Sophia would be resolving. The spaceship would also be using the docking systems for other course refinements. They only had one shot at hitting their target: all technologies aboard were going to be used.

Sophia looked over the data points one more time, but still frowned.

ISAF had sent her the telemetry points she should see the power demands on the engine for the maneuvers, they didn't match with what she was witnessing on her screens.

"I'm drawing more power than I should be right now..."

She looked up at the lights but shoot her head at the absurd thought. The LEDs that provided light on the command deck were so power efficient, there was no way that was it. A single AA battery could power the lights on the flight deck for a whole day (Earth day).

"Shit! It *is* the lights," she muttered as she dove into various computer menus.

She found the hydroponics display and confirmed it was the sun-lights that were still on, feeding light to the few plants that had been sustaining her all this time.

"Sorry plants, but if I don't live, you don't live," and she cut power to the lights.

She deactivated the rest of the hydroponics systems and water recycler, and as expected, the numbers dropped down to what ISAF had originally told her to expect.

After that, it became quiet again. Sophia took the time to look outside the windows but there was nothing but inky blackness for her to look at. It reflected the silence she was bathed in.

But only for a few minutes. An alert and audible chirp guided her attention back the *Odyssey*'s systems.

```
====================================
```

NOTE – BURN IMMINENT

```
====================================
```

PRESS ENTER TO CANCEL BURN
YOU HAVE 5... 4... 3... 2... 1...

```
====================================
```

NOTE – BURN INITIATED

```
====================================
```

Sophia felt the rumble begin again. She felt pressed slightly against her seat. It wasn't like accelerating in a fancy car, but it was a strange feeling none-the-less – one she only experienced in burns now.

"Burn initiated. On time. Semi-major axis adjusting... Roll program active. RCS active."

The RCS thrusters started to fire furiously for fine course corrections. They sounded like there was hail falling on the spacecraft but Sophia continued to read off the data she was seeing.

"Down 3, 200 left... Down 1, 100 left correcting back to right."

The furious bursts of thrust from the RCS continued.

"Down 2 on center line.... Down 1, on center line. 2 roll, drift to right, correcting back to left..."

Another alarm sounded. It was the radar.

```
====================================
```

WARNING

OBSTACLE DETECTED

=====================================

ALTERNATE COURSE PLOTTED –

ACCEPT NEW COURSE Y/N

    N

COMMAND OVERRIDE REQUIRED

ENTER PIN:

    ****

OVERRIDE ACCEPTED

ACCEPT NEW COURSE? Y/N

    N

ARE YOU SURE? Y/N

    Y

COURSE CORRECTION REFUSED

A few minutes later, Sophia again had to endure another set of alarms.

=====================================

CAUTION – NO DOCK DETECTED

=====================================

Sophia closed her spacesuit's visor.

Moments later, the *Odyssey* started to get very nervous and blared a vocal alarm started to sound:

"WARNING – VELOCITY"

"WARNING – VELOCITY"

```
===================================
```

WARNING

COLLISION IMMINENT

```
===================================
```

"Our guests tonight are two people that have spent some of the longest time living away from Earth, cumulating a total of a full year on the surface other celestial bodies, and 3 years in deep space. Now they are back on Earth and it gives me great pleasure to say that they are here with us tonight, please welcome Doctors Becky and Xavier Lange."

On cue, the local jazz band started playing and the crowd stood up clapping and cheering as Becky and Xavier walked onto the stage. Becky was dressed in a beautiful silky black dress that changed to a deep blue color as it waved and fluttered under the light that danced over it. Xavier wore a simple black suit with a blue tie that matched Becky's dress.

The host of the Late Night Show, Stephen Colbert stood up and gave a hug and kiss to Becky before shaking Xavier's hand with a beaming smile as the crowd continued their cheers and loud clapping. Becky and Xavier smiled and waved at the audience.

"Oh I'm going to say hi to this guy," laughed Xavier, pointing to a little boy in the front row who was extending his hand to the two guest stars.

Holding Becky's hand, Xavier walked up to the boy in the audience and with the rest of the crowd cheering, Becky and Xavier shook the hands and hugged some of the people adulating and adoring the two astronauts in the front row. The boy high fived Xavier while the public was still supremely excited to see the people whose titles were synonymous to intelligent, brilliant, humble, explorers and most importantly: rare, unique and extraordinary. Xavier had already known this about Becky for a long time, but he was happy to see the spectators agree with him here.

Returning to the stage, Xavier waved to Becky to sit closest to the comedian's desk as they took their seats to the continuing claps of the spectators and the jazz band slowly faded away their music to allow the interview to begin.

Xavier undid the button to his suit, which was a relief. He never knew whether or not to keep it buttoned or not while standing. Becky knew he preferred the suit jacked to be unbuttoned, but proper etiquette said the middle button should be formally buttoned up while standing.

"Wow," continued Colbert. "You seem, to be popular," laughed Colbert, pointing to the audience that was giggling and excited to see the two astronauts. "You know. That's a real superstar move, folks who can take their time with the audience like that. Not everyone can do that; that is truly a skill what you guys did there."

"Oh we cut that down," laughed Xavier and everyone else. "We just didn't want to mess your time."

"Well played," laughed Colbert. "Of course, Becky, you've been here with us in New York before, welcome back! We're so happy to have you again here on the show."

"Thank you, yes, thank you," smiled Becky.

"Three thousand people I've interviewed and you're the only person who's ever come into the rewrite room and said: 'hi I'm Becky Lange, I'm very happy to be here.' I thought: 'this person is looking for a job interview, obviously.'" Becky, Xavier and the audience laughed. "I think it was a little over a year ago that you came on?"

"That's right," nodded Becky.

"And Xavier, welcome! It's really exciting to have you on for the first time."

"Thank you."

"We were looking to interview just you but you insisted that Becky come with you: why was this?"

"Well I know that success is due in no small part to those around you so I thought it only appropriate to have those who helped me get to where I am today, regardless of how infinitesimal my successes are. And Becky is of course the one who helped, and she has been here before so I thought she'd be the easiest to convince to come along and accept your invitation. To be honest, she was my coach for what to expect here - I have to admit you guys have quite an enterprise here. It makes ISAF look like an amateur radio station."

The audience laughed.

"Well thank you so much for being here. Ok. So," paused Colbert. "You guys are known for being iconic along with all your fellow astronauts. Is that what you like to call yourselves? Astronauts? Well I think your Russian counterparts are cosmonauts, right? And the Chinese are taikonauts?"

"That's right," agreed Xavier.

"The Russians don't really care," laughed Becky. "They just called themselves Russian, at least in my experience..."

Colbert and the audience laughed.

"Well and so that's the question, is this how you like to be referred to? For example, we introduced you two as astronauts when you walked in but is there something else you believe you be preferable?"

"I think Xavier would like to be called His Imperial Presidency Doctor Master Lange, but I just said *no*."

"You should get a business card with that," laughed Colbert.

"You know, I wish I could get a business card, but everywhere we go now, people already know us," smiled Xavier. "There's no point in having cards."

"Cards are too old school anyways. So you are ok with the title astronaut?"

"I am," commented Becky.

"I guess I actually thought for the crew of the *Odyssey* and those who are traveling to other worlds exploring, the term explorer could also be applied. But I think astronaut is still very appropriate," replied Xavier.

"Ok, yeah, that's true," agreed Colbert. "That makes sense for those exploring. Xavier, you just came back from an exploration mission, yourself? The Moon?"

"Yep, but it was a pretty quick trip compared to Becky here."

"Oh how long was your 'vacation' on the Moon?" asked Colbert sarcastically.

"I was on the Moon for seven months."

"Seven months? So you spent more time on a moon than Becky did?"

"I suppose I did."

"Do you guys ever argue over who's moon was better?"

The crowd and Langes all laughed.

"I think Becky gets the gold star on that one," conceded Xavier. "You have Jupiter to look up to, ice skating and a future for skiing out there..."

"Well," interrupted Becky, "the Moon here does have Earth to look up to and near instantaneous communications with home," she continued with a more serious tone. "That's something that really needs to be emphasized and that I think both Xavier and I want to convey is simply that you don't realize how alone we are as a species.

Ignoring whether or not there are aliens out there, we don't interact with other animals at all; we only interact on an intellectual level with humans, and I think it's important to remember that connection we all have with each other. So as we continue to explore the rest of the universe, we need to do it together."

"Together?" laughed Colbert. "Oh believe me, I would love to come with you guys. Just make sure ISAF gets my application, will you? Xavier, at least you return without having to correct history about who the first to land on the Moon was."

The audience laughed. After the *Odyssey* removed Dr. Montsegur's ship from being a threat, the daring rescue plan and actual reality of the landings on Europa was revealed. Both the *Odyssey* crew and *Otkrytiye* crews had shut off their clocks after landing before stepping on the surface of Europa. No one would be able to exactly tell at what time they had landed, since there were no live communications. Both spacecraft reported back to Earth that they had landed at the exact same time. ISAF had simply lied about that detail to prevent any suspicions from fueling Dr. Montsegur's paranoia and surveillance, in order to keep him unaware of the plot to disarm him. Only after the return to Earth were the ISAF team and Russian teams able to confirm that no one would ever know who landed first: therefore, they all landed together.

On the other hand, Neil Armstrong was the first person to ever walk on the Moon, so Xavier Lange had no similar correction to history made.

"But answer this for me," continued Colbert. "Future vacations. I'm assuming that now that you are both back on Earth, for good now, I hope... Wait that's a good point: what is it about our planet that makes you want to leave it so much?" The audience laughed before Colbert continued with his question. "So now that you're back, where in the *world* are you ever going to go for a vacation that you think is even worth it?"

The audience laughed and Becky and Xavier did too.

"Well, I think being away for so long makes you appreciate any place on Earth," replied Xavier.

"Any special vacations planned?" nudged Colbert.

"Well we have a vacation planned with the children," answered Xavier, "but it's a private event and we'll just be showing the children familiar, home sites."

"Yeah, we'll be taking about three weeks to ourselves," added Becky. "It's going to be very nice to just have nothing to worry about or do. Just snuggle and spend time together," she added, looking at her husband who smiled back at her.

The crowd awed.

"We're also taking time to get the kitchen renovated while we're gone," added Xavier. "Just before coming here we went to the Ikea in Brooklyn to figure out what we liked."

"Oh you simpletons," gasped Colbert. "Such planetary problems, going shopping at Ikea, fixing up kitchens," he added theatrically. He then continued over the laughter of the audience, "I'm assuming this wasn't too much trouble for the likes of you to figure out, so what were some of the toughest moments in your career? Becky?"

Becky thought for a moment before answering:

"The darkest moments have been challenges of the flight. Problems in the spacecraft that required the very best of my abilities and those of my associates and perhaps a little help from Divine Providence. In any case those moments were followed by periods of brightness when you realize that you are able to conquer the problems."

"Xavier?" asked Colbert.

"Um... I would venture choosing a kitchen at Ikea," he smiled and the audience erupted in laughter. "But more seriously, I would have to say making the choice to make the unpopular choice. Being alone in your conviction that what you are doing is the right decision."

"Until you went to Ikea," added Colbert. "So Xavier, after stepping onto the Moon, real quick, because we asked the same thing to Becky when she stepped onto Europa... and I'm not quite sure how to ask this question... When you first stepped on the Moon, did it strike you as you were stepping...that you were stepping on a piece of the Earth, or sort of what your inner feelings were, whether you felt you were standing on a desert or that this was really another world, or how you felt at that point?"

"It's a stark and strangely different place, but it looked friendly to me and it proved to be friendly."

The audience started to clap, which surprised Xavier and Becky a little bit.

"Xavier, did you ever think in a million years you would get to do that? Walk on the Moon?"

"No. I didn't think I'd ever do that. Nor be on this show."

The audience laughed.

"So," continued Colbert as he placed a large photograph on his desk, "this is a photograph of each of you in your EVA, is that right, EVA?" The two astronauts nodded in agreement and Colbert continued. "EVA suits. Sorry, what's EVA again?"

"Extra-Vehicular Activity," answered Becky.

"We're going to stick to EVA," continued Colbert focusing on the photograph again. "So this is a picture of each of you in your EVA suits, Dr. Lange in his lunar clothing and Dr. Lange in her Europa suit. They both look really different, and I'm assuming that's because of the different environments, the Europa one in this bright orange compared to the simple white for the Moon, but the two of you show the distinct smudges of lunar soil on your knees. Did you fall down on the surface or kneel?"

The crowd laughed.

"You know what," laughed Becky, "I think I did fall." The audience also laughed. "I mean it's a moon covered in ice, what did you expect?"

"Was that the only time you slipped?" asked Colbert.

Becky paused: "No," she smirked.

The audience laughed.

"Alright, alright," chuckled Colbert. "So you have an excuse: you lived on an ice-cube. What's yours Xavier?"

"Um. I jumped a little too high," he said with a smile that showed he was slightly embarrassed.

"You jumped too high?" asked an incredulous Colbert.

"Yes. So the Moon, as you might remember, only exerts one sixth the pull of gravity compared to Earth, so one day, while leaving the hab, I thought I would just see how high I could jump, and I got pretty high, but on one of my landings I didn't land properly and instead landed on my knees - which you see dirty on that photograph. When I came home, or back into the hab, I swapped suits to make sure I didn't use a potentially damaged one anymore, and brought this one back to Earth with me."

"How high did you get?"

"I'd rather not say, I think ISAF is right now scrambling to find a punishment in the regs, and I don't want to add unauthorized launch to that list if I give an altitude."

The audience and Colbert laughed.

"Xavier, I know Becky is a bona-fide American," and Colbert paused before thinking of a way to word the question: "do you still view yourselves as American, or having lived offworld, do you think that astronauts transcend such nationalistic boundaries?"

"Well I think that when you're in space, just like I assume on the high seas, we're bound to help each other regardless of nationalities. And there is no culture, no way of life to defend in space, no territory or shrine or religious ideology since they don't exist out there: it's only what we take with us. So yes," agreed Xavier, "astronauts, through their responsibilities and just in space in general, are above nationalistic boundaries. And I think Becky had already mentioned this but as we move into deeper and deeper space, we only have those we're with: there's no direct communication with anyone else other than the crew on your spacecraft so it's going to create a new culture: a non-Earth, space-colonist culture. One that is built by the experiences of the crew, much like our cultures today are remnants of old settlements from hundreds or thousands of years ago that were separated from each other through long, communication delays. The way our cultures today coalesce is through communications."

"Interesting, yeah so you're saying that right now our national boundaries are not as significant as they were, say fifty years ago?"

"Well I think we all know they're not. Some countries like the US and China and Russia still cling to those ideas of sovereignty but we see it clearly through Europe and the African Union and even ISAF that we can keep our cultures without borders, and that is the way toward a peaceful future. We've created a space agency that flies people from various countries to the Moon and beyond. If Humans want to survive and establish future offworld colonies, the economic policies regarding the sale of milk or the production of some crop in Russia or France or the United States are going to be completely irrelevant. Pride in a system is traditionally born out of reflex and simply exists because it's what you're familiar with and therefore what you think must be right."

"That's true – I hadn't looked at it with that perspective," nodded Colbert. The host then returned to a more lighthearted comment: "So not an American?"

Xavier paused and smiled at Becky: "Well of course I'm an American, by nationality, but I think nationality is not an accurate measure of who you are and where you fit in the world. Culture would be more appropriate. So culturally, I fit with those who are ok to live on either coast of the United States and Canada, Australia, Japan and even Western Europe. I share more agreements with those regions than I do with other regions of the United States for example."

"Ok so you think that astronaut nationality is not dictated by the country they're from but the cultural background?"

"Well I think this could really devolve into a long sociological lesson but yes, the more educated and culturally diverse you are, the less nationalistic pride matters; the understanding about the complexity of human interaction – not necessarily how they work but just being aware of the incredible complexity, and how no one culture or mythology is superior becomes apparent. Human rights, focused interests instead of pride are what the focus is. And astronauts are obviously very focused, so country bickering takes a back seat."

"So you two have slightly different perspectives, that's so interesting."

"Oh we talked about this a few times in the past, back to when we met," smiled Becky.

"Wow. I'm actually glad you brought up when you met because I wanted to ask you guys about that, but we'll get to that later. Real quick, because you've already proven you can work with people from a variety of different people and nationalities, was there anything – any message, that either of you, wanted to say, while you here? Or ask?"

"Uh... I don't know. Does anyone have any questions?" asked Xavier.

"Oh... Yes. We have an audience," said Colbert. The audience laughed when he made a grimace that showed he wasn't even aware. "We usually don't like to interact with them – it makes them feel human and a part of the show," he added sarcastically to more laughter. "Who's got a question?"

Hundreds of hands in the crowd skyrocketed into the air making Becky and Xavier laugh, Becky nestling her nose into Xavier's shoulder as they chuckled.

"Oh boy," mumbled Colbert. "Curse your popularity... Ok, you sir, in the back with a decidedly bright orange t-shirt. Good choice, that made me pick you."

The man stood up and was handed a microphone by a stage aid.

"So, um, Dr. Lange..."

"Which one?" smiled Xavier with the audience giggling.

"Oh," laughed the man. "You, sir."

"Call me Xavier, just to keep it simple. This is Dr. Lange," he added, pointing to Becky. "Just so any of you guys in the audience don't get too friendly and get any ideas," which elicited some laughs. "Sorry, go ahead."

"Uh, Xavier, the *Odyssey* Blu-ray showed that throughout the start of your relationship and while Becky was traveling to Europa, you were so romantic. And, um, I think we'd all love to know, Misses doctor Lange, what romantic thing did you do to pay Xavier back for refusing a shot to Jupiter and staying on Earth?"

Becky leaned in thinking quickly before responding.

"Well, I mean, how do you pay back someone for something like that? But, uh, I don't know. I'm working on something."

Xavier jumped in: "She pays me back every day just by being my wife so that's fine."

The crowd awed and made other romantic sounds, making Xavier feel very awkward.

"O-Kay..." he simply groaned, making Becky smile and hold his hand.

Another woman in the audience was handed the microphone to ask her own question:

"All I can say is, if I had Xavier, he would have a free pass to do anything. I mean if I lucked into that... he could do anything. Anything."

Becky hesitated for a moment: "I'm sorry. Is there a question?"

"Uh, no," replied the woman before handing the microphone to the stage aid.

Another microphone had already been handed to another woman who also stood to ask her own question.

"I have a question for Xavier and Becky," started the woman. "Everyone that watched the Blu-ray that was mentioned before sees how much you love each other and how you're soul mates. So, Becky, sorry, Dr. Lange, why did you leave your family on Earth to go to Europa? Don't you regret your choice for simply abandoning the people you love?"

"Wow," interrupted Xavier. "I know the question was directed at Becky, but I'd like to start with an opening line here if I may? Becky didn't abandon anyone: she left knowing that Adeline, Thomas and myself were behind her every step of the way. I'll be honest: at first, I didn't handle that very gracefully. I didn't want to risk everything that we had. But it was far riskier to not allow her to leave Earth. Becky and I shared the same dream before we had ever met so in a sense, that dream was older than our relationship – than our own children. The simple and unambiguous fact is this: when you love someone, you help them reach those dreams. You support them. No matter what. That doesn't change if it means you have to take a business trip to another country for a week or go off-world for a few years. Because the end result is that if they don't go, then you stood in their way and I know I couldn't have lived with the thought of having selfishly asked her to stay here for me. We have our entire lives with the children ahead of us. And you would do anything for your children, I would do anything for Becky." The mood was much more serious now, but Xavier continued. "Besides, I also left the planet to live away from them. It was shorter, yes, but I'm even more to criticize since I knew how hard it was to have someone you love be so distant. But Becky leaving on the *Odyssey* mission was selfish for me anyways; do you know how cool I was to say my wife was on Europa?"

The crowd laughed easing the tension that had been created by the question that Becky Lange had yet to answer.

The audience soon fell silent again as it looked like Becky was hesitating to say something. The explorer had not expected Xavier to answer so decisively for her. It had almost been rude to the woman asking, but the questioner did have it coming after asking such a question to her in this public forum. Regardless, Becky was still emotional over the question and what Xavier had said: Becky had abandoned her family on Earth. The risks were enormous; the world could have ended while she was in transit to the Jovian moon because of Dr. Montsegur's plan to unleash an asteroid. Becky could have, herself, died in any myriad of ways (although she agreed that it was most likely from some of the food the Russians fed her during the return trip). She could have left Xavier alone to raise their two children. Children growing up without a mom because she had instead preferred to leave for to the stars. Xavier never hesitated though. He had an understanding of the challenges of the voyage and yet continued to pressure her to go forward with it. They had, in the grand scheme, held very few talks about the mission. Becky thought back to one of the four talks they had together, in the backyard of their house next to the outdoor fireplace. Xavier had covered Becky in a blanket and sat in the chair next to her before sternly telling her: "there's no point in really dragging this out: you're going. End of story. Period, dot. That's it." They talked about it one more time for her to have the last word, which made her smile internally.

"You're right," started to speak Becky. "I did leave my family behind and in a sense, I did betray my responsibility as a mother and a wife." Xavier cringed at the responsibility comment. "But that didn't happen when I launched from Earth, it happened when I applied to ISAF or when I accepted the astronaut slot. I know that there are three, very formative, very crucial years, of my children's lives that I will never be able to say I witnessed. But please do me a favor: in ten years, please ask the same question again to my children. The children were the ones that will be impacted and will be best positioned to judge my actions. Most of us can expect to live a natural life up to about 90 or 100, but let's say 80 to be conservative. That means I will die when Adeline is about 48. That means I will have missed about 7 percent of her life. I will agree with you ma'am, that this number is too high. But I will not comment on whether or not I *regret* being on the Europa mission. And you obviously know how Xavier feels about this. The important thing is that we're back on Earth and reunited. And we have a life ahead of us

– one that may not be long enough, but that we intend to maximize," she concluded, holding Xavier's hand and looking into his eyes.

"You know you're in the company of scientists and smart people when they start throwing out percentages to you," laughed Colbert to ease the tension. The host decided to end the Q&A, fearing another loaded question like this. Fortunately, the audience also laughed and the crowd clapped ferociously. "So this was just brought up with your relationship so I'm going to use that as a good lead in: you two are obviously some of the most famous astronauts in the world being the first married couple to be assigned to the space program. So how did this, this *thing* you guys have here, come to be?"

"Um....," hesitated Xavier. He didn't want to correct Colbert on television, but he also didn't want to dishonor those who were a part of the space program. "So I think you meant we're the first married astronauts, right?"

"That's right," smiled Colbert, instantly catching on. "Right because there are plenty of folks in the space program, and I'm sure a few of them are married."

"Yeah," smiled Xavier in relief. "So yes, we are the first to be astronauts. And yes, it takes a lot of people to get astronauts to space and while we are the stars of the show, it's very obvious that we as astronauts are simple switch monkeys. The ships fly themselves and rely on complex calculations ran by folks here on Earth who are a part of the space program."

"Switch monkeys," laughed Colbert. "So you two love monkeys met in San Francisco, I think, right?'

"That's right," agreed Becky. "We were both staying at a Sheraton close to Fisherman's Warf and Xavier was receiving a free drink because of his super-highbrow-snobby-elitist..."

"Loyalty rewarding," groaned Xavier.

"...status," continued Becky. "And he didn't want it so he simply gave it to me, because I was waiting in line to get my own drink."

"So you just took it?"

"No. No that would have been weird, but he insisted that he wasn't going to drink it. And then I think... What did you say? I think he said something to the effect of 'how about you take this glass of wine as a regular guy-buying-you-a-drink moment.'"

"And she said: no!" added Xavier.

The audience laughed.

"I said no, but then he corrected himself and said 'or not, that's cool, too,' and at that point I rolled my eyes and I think I finally agreed. And so we sat down and I had a glass of wine, he didn't and we just started to talk. And here we are now."

"Here you are now!" laughed Colbert. "After going to the moons of our Solar System and back, here you are now," he sarcastically added. "So obviously the thought of having to go to Europa and the Moon is a big decision to make. How did you two come to the agreement that these were missions you would go on?"

"Well I don't think there ever was much of a discussion about it," replied Xavier, looking at Becky for confirmation. "We pretty much knew that we would support each other going to space."

"There were," added Becky, "for each of us individually, real internal discussions about the children and whether or not we should go, but I think the moon-shots were fairly benign decisions."

"So you supported each other 100%?"

"A hundred percent," agreed Xavier.

"I'll be the first to admit that it's not always like this," continued Becky. "I know Xavier has had to make a couple sacrifices on some matters and philosophies in the past, and he's been sweet enough to do that to make sure that I haven't had to do that, or compromise too much," she smiled warmly at Xavier.

"That's a selfish process," added Xavier. "Making sure that Becky can be happy and live life as she thinks will make her happy can only work to my benefit."

"I wonder if anyone else has stumbled on that," mumbled Colbert. "So ISAF hasn't had to deal with you two bickering?"

"Oh they have," groaned Xavier. "Fo'sho. Yeah, the reason why two spacecraft were built to go to Europa was because they knew they would have to separate us," he joked.

"That's actually an interesting point, have you two ever thought of going to space together?"

"For now we can't," replied Xavier.

"You can't?"

"The rules prevent us, as family members, to fly together. It's the same thing with pilots on airplanes, for example: married couples can't be pilots on the same plane. But if the rules change, we could maybe take a little lunar trip next door, together. Probably not though," he corrected himself. "There's not much biology to do on the Moon."

"Yes there is!" replied Becky with a giant smile. "And I would like to go to the moon with Xavier, but I don't think I would go on the same rocket. I would meet up with him there, but not fly with him there, it's just too risky."

"Too risky? For who?" grinned Colbert.

"Oh dangerous, I meant," clarified Becky. "Something could still go wrong with the rocket and if that's the case, we don't want to orphan the children in one fell swoop. It's still riskier than flying."

"Interesting. So, how do you guys manage being in these amazing places in our galaxy without each other?"

"Well the same way others manage," replied Xavier. "We're not the *only* married astronauts."

"That's true," laughed Colbert. "I guess Neil Armstrong had to deal with his wife not being with him when he first landed on the Moon in 1969."

"In fact, having a relationship with a fellow astronaut has pros and cons," added Becky.

"How so?"

"Well on the one hand," replied Becky, "you understand the pressures associated with the training or the schedule or the change in plans. You can talk about technicalities without having to dumb it down or like that; you can even use acronyms freely, which really helps in keeping in touch. I think if you can talk to your significant other about what's bothering you at work, it can help."

"And on the other hand," replied Xavier, "you understand the pressures associated with the training or the schedule or the change in plans."

"Wait, that's what she just said," replied Colbert.

"Yeah, and since she also understands all these pressures, she knows when you're just being melodramatic about something at work. You can't over-exaggerate an issue at the office to receive some empathy or compassion. It's just 'oh please, get over it.'"

The audience laughed and Colbert nodded his head in agreement.

"So before we finish here," continued Colbert, "I just wanted to let everyone know, even though Xavier, I guess you wanted to remain anonymous, I'm sorry, but you two gave the studio a large donation, I believe $10,000?"

The crowds started to cheer and clap.

"That's right," answered Becky with Xavier nodding in the background.

"Well... Thank you," continued Colbert, which elicited laughs. "But why?"

Becky turned to Xavier for him to answer.

"Well we noticed that comedy usually is a cure all. There are few events in the world, from politics to troubles in life, that can't be cured by comedy on some level. You need to laugh in the world, and we thought we could either give to a very specific, localized event that won't help or we could try to have it percolate to as many people as possible without losing quality. And that's how we decided that comedy was it: it's easily available to everyone and we want to make sure it stays that way."

The audience again started to clap.

"Well that was very generous," continued Colbert over the clapping before shouting to the crowd: "Explorers and astronauts Becky and Xavier Lange, everyone. Thank you so much for coming!"

Chapter 19

She had been in another cylindrical machine that pressurized and flew faster than any animal could. The flight back to Houston was fairly quiet, and Becky Lange was now again in their luxury car, being driven home.

Looking outside the window into the night suburbs, Lange focused on the light sound of the rain falling on the windows of their car. The light from lamp-posts refracted. It was a sight she hadn't seen in a long time.

The interplanetary traveler thought it was ironic that she was again finding herself traveling home. She had been traveling home for the past year; since launching from Europa. There would be no welcoming committee when she would return to her home this time, though. The children should already be asleep. And even though she was still with Xavier, they were still working on restoring their relationship and falling in love with each other again. Three years apart in this modern society was difficult and the damage would take time to repair.

She thought back to her actual return from Europa. Re-entry day.

The Earth Return Vehicle (ERV) named Phaeacian was right where it was supposed to be when the *Otkrytiye* arrived in Earth orbit, and docked to the interplanetary mothership. The original crew of the *Odyssey* left the *Otkrytiye* and boarded the Phaeacian while the Russians and Indians boarded their own Earth Return Vehicle that had arrived within the same hour. Mission designers, when developing the Europa mission, had decided that the Europa lander and mothership should stay in space instead of allowing them to return to Earth (original plans had called for a simple headshield to be strapped onto the Europa lander and presto: Earth lander). With that idea gone, there was no need for a heavy additional vehicle to be hauled around the Solar System: a ship would be launched from Earth to pick them up when they came back.

Becky smiled remembering Puff calling for an update on the Phaecian. One of the first things he had done when returning within 'live' communication range with Earth was to hack into a website. Puff had hacked into the Uber website and ordered a ride from space. The explorer then called Uber when they didn't show up on time:

"Where are you? Where ARE you? I ordered my Uber hours ago!"

The Uber rep was completely confused until they realized he was pranking them.

After undocking from the *Otkrytiye*, the two Earth-landing spacecraft took a few hours to hit their reentry point.

Like Lange was doing from the window of their Audi right now, she had stared out the Phaecian's window 4 at the gorgeous planet below her. The clouds looked impossibly thin and low to the ground. She couldn't believe how high the atmosphere went above the cloud layer so many people already thought was out of reach.

A stark contrast to the grey clouds that were whirling through her mind. Strapped inside the Phaecian spacecraft, Becky Lange was still dreading saying hello to Xavier. She tried to focus on her children. On her daughter, Adeline. Her son, Thomas. It hadn't brought better memories. The questions of how she was going to react to being with

Xavier were the same worries she had about her children: how would they react being with her?

Soon after, reality resettled into the spacecraft, taking Lange's mind off of her family. The two ERVs flew through the atmosphere as two spheres of fire. The engineers had coated the exterior of the return vehicles with a small layer of a special chemical that caused the returning spacecraft to glow like auroras in the sunset skies. For observers on Earth, it was a magnificent sight. Magical.

Seven minutes later, the parachutes deployed and small motors steered the spacecraft against the wind toward the landing pads before retro-rockets ignited, illuminating the sunset-bathed landing pads, surrounded by hundreds of thousands of people. The two spacecraft landed within 8 seconds of each other. It was called an on-time, on-target landing. Four lights on one of the panels next to the words 'Gear Strut 1, 2, 3, 4' illuminated.

"Contact light," called out Hugo.

"MECO," responded Puff.

The lander came to rest on its legs, the booster engines shut off, the smoke quickly dissipating.

"Drop," continued Puff, giving the call expected that the heat from the retro-rocket engines was dissipating quickly, as expected.

"APU fuel cell activated, power-down switch to middle," read the Commander from his checklist. The middle position meant the ship would continue to run the electrical systems long enough for a ground crew to run the proper shut-down of the spacecraft, after the crew had left the ship.

"APU fuel cell is on, power-down switch is in middle," confirmed Puff.

"Center, we're stable 1, the ship is secure. This is the crew of the *Odyssey*, signing off."

Instantly, the ship started to vibrate and the astronauts started to look at the control panels in front of them. All the expected lights were on, barber-polls were locked as expected...

"It's the crowds," said Aki.

The Japanese explorer was proven right when the crew blew the hatch open and the roars of the crowd engulfed the spacecraft. Lange kicked herself for forgetting that the communications between the Phaeacian and the control center were broadcast to giant speakers in the observation park.

When the astronauts stepped out onto the landing pad, the orange sunset skies turned white, thousands of camera flashes igniting along with the flood lights bathing the landing pads.

Looking to their right, the ISAF crew saw their Russian and Indian crewmates also out on their landing site just one hundred feet away.

But Lange was only looking for specific people in the throngs of dignitaries and guests inside the reserved area. She saw one of them above the heads of others. It was Adeline, her daughter looking confusingly around. She was sitting on her father's shoulders. There was Thomas nearby!

Lange started to cry.

Sitting in the car, still staring out at the lit up strip-malls, Becky Lange smiled and sighed remembering the reunions. She was again looking forward to seeing her kids waiting for them at home with her own parents acting as guardians. But that was it. There wouldn't be the other throngs of people she had to see after having run toward her children and hugging them to the edge of suffocation. It wasn't going to be like it was a few weeks ago, where she had to greet plenty of others.

Like the ISAF controllers that got to know the crew so well over the years. Laughs and handshakes. Another friend and leader who was in a wheelchair. Hugs... Handshakes with Kings, Presidents, Prime Ministers... The Russian President proudly standing by the Russo-India team before shaking the hands of the ISAF team. A wave to the crowds, followed by louder roars and cheers. It seemed like the eyes and attention of the world were focused on the spacecraft landing pads in the Central African Republic.

There certainly would not be any newspaper titles being printed the moment her and Xavier's car would pull into their driveway, unlike the front-pages instantly printed the moment the two spacecrafts had landed after her return from Europa:

RUSSIANS AND INDIANS RETURN CREWS HOME

WELCOME HOME !

КОСМИЧЕСКИЕ СПАСЕНИЯ ВОЗВРАЩАЮТСЯ В ЗЕМЛЮ
(COSMIC SAVIORS RETURN TO EARTH)

EUROPANS ON EARTH

¡ DEVUELTO !
(RETURNED !)

नायकों आदमी के क्रैडल के लिए वापस आना
(HEROES RETURN TO CRADLE OF MAN)

WORLD WELCOMES HOME SYMBOLS OF UNITY

EXPLORATEURS EXACTE AU RENDEZ-VOUS
(EXPLORERS ACCURATELY KEEPS APPOITNMENT)

CONFETTI, HAPPINESS AND TEARS ON THANKFUL PLANET

*CREW OF LOST ODYSSEY RETURNS TO EARTH – OTKRYTIE
RESCUERS AND ISAF TEAM TOGETHER*

Lange's flashbacks ebbed away as they got closer to the familiar roads close to home and their offices. Driving down the wide avenue, flanked by modern, glass buildings and green, well-manicured grass, Lange focused on the joys of being back on Earth. The light mist pierced by lights on lampposts. The smell of humidity, the sounds of rainwater echoing on the underside of the car. The trees, thick with leaves and the pristine grass and ponds of water, manicured to perfection.

The couple momentarily turned their gaze to the monument at the center of the roundabout they were driving through.

In the center was the memorial site reserved for the heroic actions of Sophia Iolienne.

Lists & Legends

Odyssey: ISAF mothership travelling to Europa

Columbiad: ISAF lander docked to the *Odyssey* and used to land on Europa

Otkrytiye: Indo-Russian mothership travelling to Europa

Vimāna: Indo-Russian lander docked to the *Otkrytiye* and used to land on Europa

Phaeacian: Shuttle spacecraft designed to pick up passengers from orbiting vessels and returning them to Earth

Odyssey Crew-Members

Hugo Evrard   Ahmed Reygan   Trevor Puffant

Aki Suru   Sophia Iolienne Olivia Newton

Becky Lange

Otkrytiye Crew-Members

Sergei Komarov (Сергей Комаров)

Alyona Korolev (Алёна Королев)

Gopal Pande (गोपाल पांडे)

Acknowledgement

Thank you to my dear MJ for making this story possible. I know there were some struggles in the past, but just as Becky Lange persevered, you also did, which is what allowed things to end positively.

www.ingramcontent.com/pod-product-compliance
Lightning Source LLC
Chambersburg PA
CBHW032144170626
46808CB00006B/2354